Frost in the Shadows

KEITH KELTNER

CONTENTS

DEDICATION

To my daughter, Sierra.

First, I'm sorry you had to wait until my third book to be honored with a dedication. However, I had to wait for a story that didn't mention spiders, mushrooms, or sinking ships.

Second, my sincere thanks for your inspiration and humor. You also help broaden my worldview by introducing me to glorious things like Portuguese beer. Seriously, Portuguese beer—who knew?

Finally, I agree with you that chocolate-chip cookies should be soft in the middle and that everyone's playlist should include Led Zeppelin and Lynyrd Skynyrd.

Chapter 1

The Start

"Good morning, Estella. Is it Tuesday already?"

"Buenos días, Mr. Armstrong. Sí, today is Tuesday."

As she collected the dish towels for the laundry, Norman asked a rhetorical question. "You haven't seen Dillon yet this morning, have you?"

Estella politely laughed as she replied, "No, Mr. Armstrong. You know he doesn't get out of bed until noon."

Under his breath, Norman mumbled, "I'm ever hopeful that he'll get a job one day."

Estella smiled and said, "It is very nice of you to let him stay here with you after you and his mother divorced."

In another mumbled response, Norman said, "I'm not letting him stay here—he just refuses to leave!"

As Estella was leaving the kitchen, she announced over her shoulder, "Mr. Gagnon from next door is coming to the back door."

Norman rolled his eyes and took a swig of coffee before attempting to deal with his pesky neighbor. "Hello, Bernie. What brings you by so early on this uninviting morning—to the back door no less?"

"As I've told you before, my name is Bernardo—not Bernie! As for coming to your kitchen entrance, I wouldn't have to resort to such brazen steps if you would answer my calls."

Norman stood in the doorway refusing to invite his guest inside. "What seems to be the problem today? Is the hedge not trimmed straight enough? You need the name of someone to come and bale your front yard?"

Annoyed, Bernardo replied firmly, "You know good and well that your fence is on my property. I want to know when you plan to correct this!"

"Well, Bernie, I'll tell you what I'm going to do. I'm going to find me a licensed surveyor and determine the exact location of the property line. Then, and only then, will I consider what actions should be taken."

Bernardo replied, "I've already had it surveyed, and it shows you need to move your fence up to six feet in some places."

"Oh, you've had it surveyed? Well, send me the paperwork, and I'll look it over."

Not waiting for a response, Norman politely added, "Make sure to latch the gate back when you leave."

Bernardo started to ask a question, but Norman shut the door on him, drowning out the annoyance.

After getting ready for work, Norman came bounding down the stairs and got his briefcase as Estella handed him his coffee for the road.

"Mr. Armstrong, may I ask you a big favor?"

"What is it, Estella? Do you need an advance on your pay or something?"

"No, Mr. Armstrong. It's a personal request."

As he quickly glanced at his watch, he told her, "Can you ask me quickly? I'm running a little late."

"No, I'm sorry. You're too busy. I'll ask some other time."

Norman took a deep breath and calmly encouraged her to speak her mind.

"Well, Mr. Armstrong, you see, it's like this—my mother is moving up here from Chile."

He started to walk towards the front of the house as she followed close behind. "I see, so what? Does she need a job, a work visa, what?"

"Oh no, nothing like that. She needs a place to stay for a week until her townhouse is ready for her."

Confused, Norman stopped in his tracks as he turned towards Estella.

Estella briefly laughed nervously as she continued. "The room in the back would be all she needs, and it's only for a few days."

Norman just stood there looking at her blankly.

Assuming he was trying to come up with some type of tactful rejection, she preemptively said, "We'd put her in a hotel, but there is some big technology convention in town that week, and all the hotels are full. I don't have room for her at my house, and my sister has cats, and my mother is allergic…"

Norman politely stopped her and asked, "When is your mother going to be here?"

"She'll be here next week."

"And it's only for a week?"

"Yes. Uh, two weeks, at the most! You won't even know she's around."

Again moving towards the front door, Norman agreed to let Estella's mom use his guest room for no more than two weeks. Estella rejoiced as she exclaimed, "I don't know how we can ever repay you!"

As he walked out, he said, "Just have her give me another bottle of that Chilean wine that you got for me last Christmas."

"You won't regret it, Mr. Armstrong!"

As he headed down the walkway, he mumbled under his breath, "Too late, I already regret it."

As he neared the sidewalk, he saw one of the younger teenagers from the neighborhood, Blake Stuart, headed his way. Norman quickened his pace and tried to avoid eye contact, but as he turned onto the sidewalk to make his escape, he nearly ran into the post lady. She gasped at the near-collision as she steered her little mail cart onto the grass.

"Mr. Armstrong! Please watch where you're going!"

Startled, and a little annoyed that his escape route was blocked, he tried to make the most of it. "Oh, hello, Ms. Scharper. Sorry about that. I didn't see you there."

Her cold stare made him uneasy as he tried to walk around her. "You are looking as lovely as ever."

She started to grin a little at the compliment even though she knew it was anything but sincere. However, as soon as she started to reply, he spoke again.

"Yes, there is such a beautiful glow about you. When are you due?"

Her look immediately changed to mild rage as she gritted her teeth to reply. "My baby boy was born nine weeks ago!"

Norman tried to offer some sort of apology but quickly saw that there was no escape for him. He just nodded and said, "Oh, I see." Then, capitalizing on Blake's presence, he turned and started to talk to him. "Blake, how are you doing? So nice of you to stop by."

As he got some space between him and the now-irate Ms. Scharper, he dropped the pretense and told Blake, "Listen, I'm really late for work. Maybe you can swing by some other time?"

Blake was an awkward and insecure 15-year-old who, for some reason, liked to talk to Norman. This was rather odd since Norman very seldom had any time for anyone, much less a pimply-faced teenager.

As Norman got into his car, Blake asked timidly, "Maybe you'll buy some candy bars from me later? We're selling them for this year's band camp."

Norman just smiled without answering and drove off.

On the way into the city, he received a call on his Bluetooth from Nigel Tilghma, a pesky supplier of bulk products to various businesses Norman owned.

"Good morning, Norman! This is Nigel, and I have a special offer for you."

Not wanting to hear anymore about it, Norman blurted, "No, thank you."

"Railroad ties. Your cost would only be two dollars each delivered right there to your building supply store over on Macon."

Constantly skeptical of any deal Nigel offered, Norman replied, "Two dollars each—what's the catch?"

"Norman, buddy! This is a great opportunity for you. You buy for two and sell for 14. If you had markups like this on everything you sold at all of your businesses, you'd finally be able to buy that island in the South Pacific you've always wanted."

"Come on, Nigel. I know you. There is more to this story. Either tell me now, or I'm hanging up."

The two men played cat and mouse over the deal for several more minutes before Norman made an offer. "I'll take 100 railroad ties and see how fast I can sell them. How soon can you deliver them?"

Nigel laughed and then got serious, "Norman, my friend, this is a bulk sale. You have to buy the whole load to get the two-dollar price. I can't just sell you 100 ties for that price."

"See? There's always more to the story. How many railroad ties are there in this load of yours?"

Again, Nigel chuckled lightly before answering. "It's a container ship of 500,000 slightly used railroad ties."

Shocked, Norman nearly rear-ended the car in front of him. "Are you out of your mind? I'm lucky if I sell 100 in a month!" He started mumbling as he calculated in his mind. "It'd take me over 400 years to sell that many ties!"

Nigel started to change his sales pitch slightly, but Norman had heard enough. "Hey, Nigel, I have to hang up now, I'm going into a tunnel." After a few incoherent sounds and a lame attempt at mimicking some static, Norman hung up.

Pulling into his parking space at the office, Norman noticed his brother's car parked nearby. Frederick was clearly the spoiled sibling who was never held accountable for anything. He spent eight years getting his bachelor's degree and then another four getting his law degree. It was a total waste of time since he finally stopped trying to pass the bar exam after failing it for the seventh time. After a string of failed jobs, he seemed to have found a decent job as a clerk in a law firm. However, he recently quit before they implemented a random drug-testing policy. Needless to say, Norman was not looking forward to speaking to his brother.

Walking through the front door, he could see Frederick sitting on a clerk's desk thumbing through the files. Guiltlessly, Frederick looked up and yelled out, "Norm! A little late this morning, aren't you? Or do you always come dragging in at this hour?"

Norman unlocked his office door and entered with his brother right behind him. "What are you doing here, Freddie?"

"I just stopped by to see how my little brother is doing. Why are you always so suspicious?'

"Freddie, this is my business. If you expect to see me here, you should make an appointment. This really isn't a good time, or place, for a family reunion."

Laughing nervously, Frederick tried to calm his brother. "Listen, Norm, I want to talk to you about a business deal. That's what you do, right? Make business deals."

Firmly, Norman replied, "I don't believe you have a clue as to what my business is, nor do I believe you could have any deal that would interest me. Now, if you please..."

Frederick stepped forward and interrupted. "I want to buy into your business!"

Stunned, Norman tried to process the bizarre proposal. Right when he was about to ask Frederick to repeat what he had just said, Patrick Harbison, Norman's business partner, walked through the open door. "Hey, Norman, I just got this idea... Oh, hello Frederick, I didn't know you were here. I'm not interrupting anything, am I?"

As Norman was about to say, "No, my brother was just leaving," Frederick blurted, "No interruption at all, just carry on as if I'm not even here."

Patrick smiled and plowed ahead. "Great, so, anyway, I see where there is a small chain of drive-through coffee kiosks up in Lynnwood and Everett that may be interested in selling. There are only seven of them currently, but they plan to open three more by the end of the year. I've been going over the numbers, and it looks like a positive return."

Annoyed that his brother hadn't left yet, and doubtful Patrick didn't have a hidden agenda, Norman suspiciously asked, "Is this those topless-barista coffee shacks?"

Patrick excitedly replied, "Yes, Too Perky Coffee—so you've heard of them!"

Frederick sat on the corner of Norman's desk and simply stated, "Oh, boy! This sounds great."

Norman shook his head slowly as Patrick continued to read off a few financial stats that seemed important to him.

Through the open door, Norman saw one of his clerks in the outer office pointing to the clock in an effort to remind him of a scheduled conference call in just a couple of minutes. He stepped towards the door as he said, "No, we are not going to buy topless anything! Now, can you please bring me the Henley contract that I asked you for yesterday? I need it for our conference call."

He then looked at his brother, pointed towards the door, and said, "Please make an appointment the next time you wish to drop by."

As he finally got the two men out of his office, he breathed a sigh of relief.

Getting situated at his desk to prepare for his call, he glanced out of the window to see his brother and Patrick in a huddle. He could not imagine what the two were talking about but guessed it had something to do with Frederick's sudden desire to become a partner.

Norman was jolted back to more immediate concerns as his phone rang for the start of his call.

By the time the call was over, both Frederick and Patrick had left. This was actually a welcome development since Norman had a lot of other work demanding his attention.

In the early afternoon, his cell began to ring. He almost answered it before looking at the caller ID, but his sixth sense prompted him to check. It was a call from Frederick's wife, Brandi. Realizing he had dodged a bullet; he slowly placed the phone down on the table without answering it. All of his previous conversations with his sister-in-law only served to raise his blood pressure and solidify his opinion that she was an opportunistic gold-digger who was extremely frustrated that she had latched her wagon onto his loser brother.

As soon as his cell stopped ringing, and anticipating that she would now call the office, he walked over to the window facing the outer office and knocked on it loudly. As soon as the clerks looked at him, he waved at them as he closed the blinds to his office. They knew what this meant.

When the office phone rang, his assistant Nadia waited until after the third ring to answer it. Promptly after her greeting, Brandi blurted, "Put Norman on!"

Nadia paused for a second before replying, "I'm sorry, I haven't seen him in the office since he waved goodbye a little while ago. May I take a message?"

Before hanging up, Brandi barked, "Forget it!"

As Norman got ready to leave, Patrick returned to the office. Patrick quickly jumped at the opportunity to pitch his idea to buy Too Perky Coffee, but Norman just shook his head. "Patrick, this idea is worse than the telemarketing phone-bot business you wanted to buy."

"Hey, that had a strong rate of return."

"For the three months before the attorney general's office in 13 states ruled them illegal. Then nine other states joined them soon afterwards. Seriously, Patrick, can't you see the inherent risks of buying a chain of topless coffee shops?"

Patrick brushed off the negativity and again started listing the favorable returns the business had been showing over the past year.

Picking up his briefcase and slowly walking towards the door, Norman looked at Patrick and asked, "Why did I ever think going into business with you would be a good idea?"

Walking backwards as he was herded out of Norman's office, Patrick replied, "Because we make such a great team! My paradigm-shifting ideas and your head for business—we make a great partnership."

"Have a good afternoon, Patrick. And forget about the coffee shops—it's not going to happen."

"Your brother thought it was a good idea."

With a smirk, Norman replied, "He would. His idea of a good business investment would be a surf shop in Montana. Either that or some business that would allow him to sit around and drink cheap beer all day."

Relentlessly, Patrick made one last pitch before Norman left. "Just go home and sleep on it. We'll talk about the growth potential tomorrow when you're in a better mood."

Norman turned to face Nadia, "Thanks for running interference for me earlier. I owe you." Nadia smiled as she nodded acknowledgement.

He then glanced again at Patrick and firmly said, "Goodbye, Patrick. I'll see you tomorrow."

His commute home was spent thinking about fighting off his business partner's efforts to buy a chain of topless coffee shops and his brother's sudden interest in his business. To drown out these thoughts, he turned on his favorite oldies radio station.

The announcer was talking about the year 1996. "In January of that year, one of the worst blizzards in U.S. history hit the eastern states killing more than 150 people... The Dallas Cowboys won their third Super Bowl in four years becoming the first NFL franchise to do so... Garry Kasparov beat a computer named Deep Blue in their second chess match... The Unabomber was arrested in a remote Montana cabin, and the Colorado Avalanche won their first Stanley Cup. Of course, it wasn't all good news in '96—that was the year our Supersonics lost to the Bulls in the NBA Championship series. It was also the year the summer Olympics in Atlanta were disrupted by the Centennial Olympic Park bombing."

More focused on business than pop culture, Norman listened more closely when the announcer mentioned that it was in 1996 that Santa Fe Railway and Burlington Northern Railroad merged to form BNSF Railway. He briefly wondered how much they spent on railroad ties back then.

The announcer continued, "The average cost of a new house that year was $118,200, and the average monthly rent was only $554. Cost of a gallon of gas was $1.22, while U.S. postage stamps sold for 32 cents each. A new car would run you about $16,300."

This caused Norman to laugh out loud and say to himself, "Wow! Things were so much better back then."

As the Tracy Chapman song "Give Me One Reason" started to play as one of the hits from that year, Norman got hung up on the line, "Give me one reason to stay here..." This prompted a heavy dose of self-reflection about his life, his business, and his direction in life. Was 47 years of age too old to set a new direction? He wondered.

Pulling into his neighborhood, he saw his stepson Dillon intentionally drive through a large puddle splashing and completely soaking Blake, who was walking on the sidewalk. Norman stopped in the road and lowered his window. Dillon pulled alongside and lowered his window as well.

"You intentionally drenched that boy! Why on earth would you do that?"

"Lighten up, old man. He'll get over it."

Dillon looked in his mirror to watch Blake's reaction to the soaking. Norman watched in embarrassment as Blake struggled to pick up the candy bars that fell out of his now soaked paper bag.

"You should go over there, apologize for your bullying, and help him pick up his stuff."

Dillion chuckled as he looked back at Norman. "Uh, no, that won't happen. I'm late meeting my friends."

Norman started to go off on Dillon's rudeness, but Dillon interrupted. "You need to get some more steaks and beer—we're all out."

With his blood pressure reaching a peak, Norman replied. "What? There were three porterhouse steaks in there just last night!"

Revving the engine slightly trying to block out Norman's protest, Dillon said, "Yeah, well, a friend came by with his dog, and they were both hungry, so we cooked them up for lunch."

Trying to process the fact that this freeloading little jerk had helped himself to his best food, not to mention had fed one of the best steaks imaginable to a dog, Norman was aghast and speechless. Before he could respond, Dillon added, "There may have been something wrong with the steak because it made the dog sick, and he pooped in the house. Don't worry; I had Estella clean it up for you."

With veins bulging in his forehead, Norman was preparing to erupt with a lengthy scolding when Dillon smiled mockingly and announced, "I'm late—gotta run!" He then sped off.

After pulling into the driveway, Norman just sat for a moment as he tried to calm down. When he got out of his car, he watched Blake's mother helping her son carry his load of candy bars back to their house. Blake must have said something to her because she gave Norman a bone-chilling stare. He just stood there expressionless before turning to go into the house.

As he reached for the door, it flew open as Estella was leaving. "Hello, Mr. Armstrong. Hope I didn't startle you. I'm all done for the day—I'll be back on Friday."

"Oh, hello, Estella. Thank you. Listen, I just heard about the dog and all, sorry about that. Dillon really should have cleaned that up himself. Actually, Dillon shouldn't even be living here in the first place."

"No problem, Mr. Armstrong. You're a nice man for letting him stay here. Are you still okay with my mom staying in the back for a week?"

After learning how Dillon had treated her, how could he say no? "Estella, it'll be fine. I'm sure it'll all work out and be over before we realize it. I mean, your mother is a nice lady like you, right?" He smiled as he said this.

"No, not really," was her response. She then smiled broadly and added, "Nobody is as nice as me, Mr. Armstrong!"

He nervously laughed as she left.

With his porterhouse steak no longer an option, he dined on a peanut-butter sandwich and, since Dillon had failed to close the bag correctly, stale chips. After rinsing off his plate, he glanced in the garbage can where he spotted the latest edition of *The Economist* magazine. Quickly retrieving it and tossing it on the counter, he got some paper towels to wipe off the soda that had spilled on it. Annoyed that it had been discarded before he had had a chance to look at it, he flipped it over to clean off the other side. As he did so, an envelope slipped out from inside the magazine.

The envelope was unlike regular junk mail and seemed to be an invitation. It was addressed to Mr. and Mrs. Norman Armstrong. Norman smirked to himself. "I've been divorced for three years now. If this is a wedding invitation from someone who doesn't know me well enough to know that...well, the price I'm willing to spend on their gift just got cut in half."

Norman ripped open the letter to discover a hand-written note paper-clipped to an invitation. The note read, "We haven't received your RSVP from the first two invitations—really hope you can make it!" He then opened the invitation to see that it was for his 30th high-school reunion at the end of the week. As he looked at his calendar, he noticed that he had no plans for the weekend. Still, it was very short notice. Then again, the note implied that this was the third invitation that had been sent to him, and he had found this one, by accident, in the trash.

Faced with conflicting emotions—upset that his mail was being tossed out before he read it and excited to possibly attend his 30th reunion—he slowly returned to his favorite chair to think. He had missed the 10th reunion because of work. The 20th reunion was in the same month as his wife's birthday, and she refused to do anything where she wasn't the center of attention. Needless to say, they didn't make that one either.

He wondered about some of his old friends and if they would be there. He smiled as he thought about his old girlfriend, Leila.

Whatever happened to her, he wondered. Did she get married? Would she be at the reunion?

Negativity started to dominate his thoughts as he realized that Ellensburg was two hours away. He'd have to get a hotel room, and at this late date, they probably would be all booked up by now. He started doubting that any of his friends would even show up. With a slight grimace, he considered that he'd come face-to-face with Chad Clapp, the only student he had actually disliked in school. He then rolled his eyes at the notion that evil Mrs. Brewer, his old English teacher, could possibly be there. On that note, he tossed the invitation onto the table and turned on the television.

After flipping through several channels, he finally stopped on a re-run of an old prison movie where three inmates were preparing to escape from Alcatraz. Having seen the movie before, he focused less on the actual dialogue and more on the aimless thoughts about people trapped in undesirable situations. He considered the careful and meticulous planning involved in planning their escape, not to mention the extreme luck required to encounter the ideal circumstances. So many various things would have to become available at just the precise time in order to escape.

His mind drifted past the actual mechanics of the escape and pondered upon the level of stress a person trying to commit such a feat would experience. The constant fear of being discovered and re-captured. Of course, there was the fear of the elements as well. Could they survive the escape?

In reality, the men who did escape Alcatraz were never found. Norman wondered if they were able to escape or did they die trying. Near the end, he fell asleep in his chair and dreamed of one of the men succeeding. In his dream, this man was able to start his life over with a fresh slate.

Norman asked himself, "When are you too old to start over?"

Chapter 2

Soft Candy

The next morning Norman kept thinking about the Alcatraz movie he had seen and continued to wonder if the convicts had successfully escaped and been able to start over with a fresh slate somewhere. As he started to fantasize about his own opportunities to change his life's direction, he heard a commotion from the edge of his back yard. Bernardo was yelling at someone while pointing to the fence that separated the two properties. Norman thought it had something to do with the property line dispute that his neighbor alleged existed between them.

With his curiosity getting the better of him, Norman walked out onto his back deck in hopes he could hear what Bernardo was saying to the other man. Shortly after walking onto his deck, Norman saw the two men emerge on his side of the hedge row with an extended tape measure. The two stopped, briefly conferred, and then sprayed an orange dot onto Norman's lawn.

Norman sipped his morning coffee as he watched the two trespassers walk several feet away from his house, stop, and spray another orange dot onto the grass. Afterwards, as Bernardo looked at the other man, he noticed Norman standing on his back porch quietly watching everything. Bernardo shouted towards Norman, "Still waiting for your surveyor to confirm what I already know!"

Norman laughed to himself as he slowly turned and went back in the house without replying.

After finishing his toast and coffee, and wanting to be a little annoying to his lazy step-son, Norman loudly dropped his knife into the metal kitchen sink and rattled his coffee mug while he washed it vigorously. He smiled in hopes that the noise had caused at least a slight disruption to Dillon's sleep.

As he got ready for work, various thoughts flashed through his head. He knew he had to get his own surveyor to determine if Bernardo was right about the property line. He then thought back 13 years when he first bought the place and how all the property lines seemed clearly marked and defined. Thinking back all this time reminded him of his move back to Washington from Colorado, where he had worked since graduating from college. It also brought back happy memories of the year he lived there before his marriage. He was happy he had kept the house in the divorce.

After getting ready for work and heading for his car, he saw where Dillon had parked behind him blocking his departure. His frustration with Dillon blinded Norman to the point he did not noticed Blake walk up to him. "Good morning, Mr. Armstrong!"

His sudden greeting startled Norman as he placed his briefcase and coffee cup in the car. "Hello, Blake. Do you enjoy sneaking up on people like that?"

"Gee, Mr. Armstrong, I have to sneak up on people because they usually run away when they see me coming."

Norman felt guilty since he was one of the folks who tried to avoid Blake if he saw him coming towards him. Walking around the back of the car to see how much of the yard he would have to drive through to get around Dillon's car, he noticed Blake was close behind with his box of candy bars. "Haven't you sold your candy yet?"

"No, sir, I'm not having much luck with this selling stuff."

Norman took a second to look in Blake's candy box. Deciding to give the insecure lad a couple of pointers on salesmanship, he reached in and picked up one of the candy bars. "Listen, kid, when you have something to sell, you need to know your product and your customer." As he gripped the sample candy bar, he noticed that it was very soft. "These things are melted! How'd that happen?"

"Well, I may have set the box too close to the stove this morning..."

Norman held one end of the candy bar as it drooped. "Who's going to buy melted candy bars?"

Looking deflated, Blake replied, "Probably the same folks who wanted to buy them before they melted—nobody."

Norman reached in the box and pulled out a second one to find it was also thoroughly melted. He could see the sense of failure on Blake's face and wanted to help boost his confidence somehow. "Maybe your mom knows some women who could use melted chocolate to cook stuff. Maybe you can find some pot-heads who'll have such a sweet-tooth that they'll buy all of your melted chocolate."

Blake looked at Norman as if to ask where he could find some hungry pot-heads, but Norman, wanting to avoid sending the young teen in search of drug users, scurried to make another quick suggestion. Looking down at the droopy candy bars, Norman chuckled as he said, "Maybe you could give a free blue pill with every purchase."

"Blue pill?"

Without thinking, Norman added, "Sure, I'm sure your dad's got a large bottle of the stuff in the medicine cabinet—trust me, I've seen your mom, so I know he's got a stash somewhere." He chuckled again until he looked up and saw the inquisitive look on Blake's face. Realizing he should have kept his thoughts to himself, he decided to abandon the sales training and just buy a couple of the bars from the boy and then be on his way.

His final comment to Blake as he got in his car was, "Listen, kid, just ignore what I just said. You'll figure out a way to sell your candy."

After jockeying around Dillon's car, he sped off to work.

Once at work, Patrick followed him into his office as he got situated. "Did you sleep on it?"

Norman gave him a puzzled look.

"Too Perky Coffee! Did you finally realize what an awesome opportunity this is? I mean, seriously, Norman, how can you pass up such a sweet deal?"

Norman stopped Patrick and said, "It's a string of topless coffee shops…"

Patrick interrupted, "Don't tell me you're offended by a couple of women's bare breasts!"

"Patrick, what offends me or not is not the issue. The issue is that our business is buying troubled businesses that have real growth potential. We work to improve these businesses' weaknesses, and then we either sell back our controlling interests to the previous owner or we sell them on the open market. You continue to tell me that these coffee shacks are making money, so why do they need us? Furthermore, why do we need them?"

Laughing, Patrick said, "Okay, so you're still warming up to the idea. I'm sure you'll come around soon enough. Meanwhile, here's another business opportunity for us: Issaquah Treasure Finders!"

"Aren't they the folks that you tell that you are looking for some vintage lunchbox with an ugly cat painted on it, and then they send their team of people out to all the flea markets, swap meets, thrift stores, and garage sales looking for it?"

"Yes! So you've heard of them?"

"Not interested."

"What do you mean you're not interested? Why not? What's wrong with this idea? They need our help to streamline their operations, their communications, their billing…"

"Patrick, seriously, do you even think about these ideas for more than a minute before you start getting worked up about them? A blind man can see that the business is far too labor intensive. The first thing we would need to do is go in and start laying people off. Do you want to start telling people that they no longer have a job just a couple of months before Thanksgiving?"

"So, you want to wait until January before we buy into that one?"

Norman, frustrated with trying to get through to his thick-headed partner, changed the subject. "Lark Hardware—do you have any legitimate reason why we shouldn't sell our controlling interest back to Marsha Lark? They have been running great for a little over a year and should do well on their own now."

Briefly considering the question, Patrick replied, "Sure, that's fine with me. The timing would be good to build up our reserves so we can make a tempting offer for Too Perky Coffee."

Speechless, Norman pointed towards the door with a determined look.

Patrick thought he might have used up all of Norman's patience for the morning and said, "I'll let you get settled. We can talk more after you've had your morning coffee."

Norman finally got settled and began to review performance numbers for a couple of their holdings. As he glanced up momentarily and looked through his office window, he saw his brother and Patrick in an involved conversation about something. Initially, Norman thought it might have something to do with Freddie's recent interest in buying his way into the business. Maybe he wants to buy a piece of Patrick's ownership in the company, he thought.

Norman was startled slightly when Nadia announced that he had a phone call.

He quickly learned that it was the owner of the dry dock where he kept his small boat. "Wow, a call from you can't be good news. What is it this time? Are you raising the storage fees again?"

The owner laughed as he asked, "Well, that depends. How much more are you willing to pay to keep your boat here?"

"You are talking about storage for a boat I rarely use. I guess the short answer is that I'm not willing to pay anything more."

Both men laughed lightly before the owner said, "Relax, there are no rate increases in the near future. However…"

Norman interjected, "Oh boy, here it comes. Let me sit down."

The owner continued, "Just to make sure we're clear, I'm calling about your 30-foot Bowrider named *Marian Rose*."

Norman acknowledged. "Yes, the *Marian Rose* is the only boat I own."

"Well, we noticed an increase in rodent activity around here, and our pest-control folks traced a couple of roof rats back to your boat. It seems several of them had a nice little nest in there with all of the food that had been left on board."

"Food? I never leave food on board. Actually, I don't think I've used my boat since the Christmas parade of boats last year. I know I only had coffee at that time, and there was no food."

"Our records show it was used several times over the summer."

"Really? Who signed it out?"

"Dillon Huff signed it out. The notes in the record said that you were out of the country, so they confirmed permission with your wife, Adrianna."

Norman took a second to process the anger that was building up inside. He then asked, "You are telling me that I have rats in my boat because Dillon left food on it?"

The boatyard owner replied, "It appears that is correct. We took the liberty of bringing the boat down from the rack so that we could eradicate the rodents first of all, and then to determine how much damage they may have caused."

"How bad can it be?"

"It's pretty bad. The rats seem to have chewed up a lot of the wiring below deck to the point that now several of the electrical instruments and lights no longer operate. Our yard mechanic found water in the oil line. This may be the result of the rats or some other issue, and then we found that the bilge pump continues to malfunction."

Norman just shook his head in disbelief. "How much is it going to cost me to fix everything?"

"It's going to be expensive since all of the wiring..." The boatyard owner paused, realizing that Norman was a bottom-line kind of guy. "We'll work up a detailed estimate and send it to you."

Trying to refocus his attention onto his work after the bad news from the boatyard, Norman walked over to Nadia's desk. "Do you have the latest month-ending report for Bink's Scoops?"

As she retrieved the file, she said, "For a chain of ice cream shops, they do fairly well."

"Yes, we will probably add another store in the spring and another one by late summer. I'm meeting with them tomorrow for lunch to discuss the details."

With an approving nod, she replied, "Not bad considering the condition of the business a couple of years ago when you bought into it."

Norman was starting to say something else when they heard the front door open. He turned to see Brandi enter. It was too late to hide—he'd been seen.

As she walked near, she spoke to Norman while glaring at Nadia. "How come I get the feeling that if I'd called from outside, I'd have been told you weren't here?"

Norman tersely asked, "What do you want, Brandi?"

"Freddie needs a job!"

"I heard the City of Bellevue is looking for storm drain inspectors for the upcoming rainy season. However, I believe they too conduct random drug tests."

Nadia tried to contain her chuckles regarding Norman's response.

Irritated at Norman's lack of seriousness, she walked towards Norman's office as she stated, "We need to speak in private!"

Norman asked Nadia to remind him about his meeting with Lark Hardware if Brandi got too long-winded. He then followed her into his office.

"This is serious! Freddie needs a job, and he does not need his brother making light of the situation."

Before he could respond, Brandi launched into a lengthy tirade as to why Norman should bring Freddie into his business and how families are supposed to be there for one another. As she continued to lobby Norman to employ her husband, Norman sat at his desk and started reading reports and making notes for his afternoon meeting. His lack of attention infuriated her.

"Are you even listening to me?"

"I'm really trying hard not to. Why, are you getting ready to say something important?"

"How do you expect us to make it without a job?"

"I don't know and really have stopped caring. Freddie had a good job, but he liked smoking pot and drinking more so he quit—he wasn't furloughed or downsized out of a job—he quit. Why? Just because he knew he couldn't pass the drug test. Therefore, his situation, and especially your situation, is none of my concern."

Defiantly folding her arms, she replied, "Why won't you even give him a chance? Are you afraid he'd do this job better than you?"

Laughing, Norman shot back. "This job is about negotiations, deal-making, and process improvement. He can't even improve his own drug use problem, and when he doesn't get his way, he sends you in here to fight his battles. No, I'm not afraid of him being better at this job than me!"

"Freddie didn't send me here! I came here because he needs a job."

Norman tilted his head and asked, "Why don't you get a job? Is this what it's all about? You're afraid you may have to get a job if Freddie can't?"

"I have plenty of money! I just don't want to tap into it. It's savings—for retirement." After a brief pause, she asked, "What's going on with that chain of coffee shops you're thinking of buying?"

Puzzled, Norman wondered what that had to do with anything they were discussing. He answered, "We're not buying any coffee shops."

With a softer tone, Brandi asked, "Really? I heard it was a very lucrative investment. Maybe you could buy it and put Freddie in charge of it."

Norman shot back, "If you think it's such a great investment and you have plenty of money, why don't you buy it and put Freddie in charge of it?"

Nadia called over the intercom, "Don't forget your meeting with Mrs. Lark."

Norman stood up, locked his desk, and gathered his files.

Brandi grew frustrated as she bellowed, "I'm not done with you!"

Norman continued walking towards the door as he calmly replied, "Well, fortunately, I'm done with you."

He felt happy with himself for being able to leave the discussion with Brandi. She had a knack for pushing all of his buttons, and he realized that his peace of mind depended upon his ability to limit his interaction with her.

As he drove out of the parking lot, he noticed his brother's car was still there even though he hadn't seen Freddie anywhere inside the office before he left. Come to think of it, he hadn't seen Patrick either. Norman briefly wondered where they were off to until he realized he needed to mentally prepare himself for his afternoon meeting.

Talking with Marsha Lark about the progress they had made streamlining the operations of the small hardware chain after her husband's death reminded Norman why he enjoyed his job so much. While Marsha's husband knew his business forwards and backwards, she had issues trying to run it the same way. She didn't want to sell it since it was always their dream to leave it to their son once he finished college.

Norman bought a piece of the business and worked to improve all aspects of the business from procurement to sales and from marketing to record keeping. With the increase in profits Marsha had earned from the improved efficiencies, she was now able to buy back Norman's share.

Of course, Norman made money on the deal compensating him for his efforts. However, for Norman, the true fulfillment was seeing Marsha succeed.

"I'm surprised your partner isn't here to participate in the final round of glory."

"Yes, well, Patrick's sorry that he couldn't make it today, but he had a previously scheduled meeting." They both knew Norman was just being polite. "I'll tell him you were sorry he couldn't make it."

Marsha was better known for her bluntness than her tact. "Don't lie to him on my account. Frankly, I'm glad he didn't show up. I always felt that you were the only one who ever took a sincere interest in helping me out. I always got the feeling he was analyzing everything in terms of what his profits would be if he were to just liquidate the business piece by piece."

Wanting to leave the meeting on a more positive note, Norman asked that Marsha contact him if she needed any assistance with the store.

Since it was too late in the day to go back to work, Norman headed home. His journey was accompanied by the sounds from the year he graduated from high school as the radio station saluted 1986. The announcer highlighted some of the major headlines of the year: "...The Space Shuttle Challenger exploded shortly after launch. The worst-ever nuclear disaster occurred as the Chernobyl nuclear power station exploded causing the release of radioactive material across much of Europe. Mad cow disease was identified and sent panic through the beef-eating world. In September of that year, we learned that all of season nine of the popular television series *Dallas* was a dream when Bobby Ewing returned to the show…"

As the announcer began to highlight the economy from that year with the average price of a new car and home, Norman got hung up thinking about the dream erasing an entire year of a television show. He said to himself, "With the Challenger explosion, mad cow, and Chernobyl, I'm sure many folks wished they could simply dream away all of 1986."

As the next song came on, Norman's mind wandered, and he considered the various events in his life that he wished he could just dream away.

When he returned to reality, he thought about the sizable chunk of change he had just made on selling his share of the Lark Hardware chain and instantly got into a great mood. Still riding the wave of euphoria from his deal when he arrived home, he had a spring in his step when he got out of his car.

"What the hell were you thinking?" The shrill voice startled Norman, causing him to jump and turn rapidly.

Standing defiantly with her fists clenched, Ms. Stuart was mad. Her veins bulged noticeably on her forehead. Norman tried to figure out how he didn't see her when he pulled in. He quickly glanced around to see if there were any others lurking around to jump out and scare him.

She continued, "It's bad enough that you allow your son to bully my boy all the time, but now you have to go and do this!"

Slowly, he mumbled a brief response. "Uh, hello there. You're Blake's mom, right?"

"Yes! Blake is my son, and I'll have you know there were no little blue pills around to help his father and me conceive him! Furthermore, his dad left us high and dry months ago and didn't leave any stash of medication around the house for Blake to tape to his candy bars."

Norman quickly paled as he realized she had somehow learned of his joking around earlier that morning. As she continued to attack him for his inappropriate comments, he became curious as to how she found out about the remarks. Did Blake tell her, or did someone else overhear his comments and tell her? Either way, he thought he might have an opportunity to allege some degree of misrepresentation or possibly missing context of the remarks.

Right when he was about to ask how she had heard about the earlier conversation, she said, "I knew that body camera would come in helpful! I just figured I would get hard evidence on your son's bullying. I never anticipated hearing someone... I mean, really! You said..."

Norman stopped her and asked, "What did you say? You equipped your son with a body camera?"

She folded her arms and firmly replied, "Yes, I did! It's the same one the police use. It's a good thing I did, or I'd have never known..."

Norman slowly shook his head as he asked, "Who does that?"

She pointed her finger at him and shouted, "Oh, no, you don't! This isn't about how I raise and protect my boy. Don't you try turning this around on me! You are the one in the wrong here, Mr. Armstrong!"

"Please, call me Norman, or even Norm, if you like."

"No, I don't like! I don't like any of it one bit! I don't like your son bullying Blake, I don't like you telling my son that I'm ugly..."

"I never actually said that you..."

"And I don't like you talking to my teenage son about sexually enhancing drugs!"

She then made a sound that was a cross between a muffled scream and an angry growl as she turned and stormed off. Norman briefly stood there as he glanced around to see if anyone else was getting ready to jump out and scare him. As he made his way to the house, he thought to himself, "Well, now I know where Blake got his skill for sneaking up on people."

As Norman started to unwind in his favorite recliner, Dillon bounded into the room, excitedly announcing, "I'm going to the Kilo Hammer concert!"

Annoyed at being startled, Norman snipped, "Sounds like a hardware convention."

"Dude, you are so out of touch. They are the hottest rock band on the West Coast!" Believing further explanations would be wasted, he just turned and started to walk away as he mumbled, "Whatever."

Sitting up straight in his recliner, Norman called out, "Dillon, I got some things I need to tell you."

Dillon faced Norman without speaking a word and gave his best uninterested stance.

Norman firmly said, "Stop bullying the neighbor kid. Do not throw my mail in the trash. Don't park behind me. And stop ordering Estella around as if she is your personal servant—she's not!"

Flippantly Dillon replied, "Is there anything else?"

"Now that you mention it, there is! You need to get a job and move out of my house before the end of the year. Is that understood?"

Dillon snapped. "You can't talk to me like this! You're not my father! My mom says I can stay here as long as I like."

Leaning forward in his chair, Norman calmly replied, "That's true—I'm not your father. Your father is only about halfway through his sentence at the federal maximum-security prison down in Atwater, California. Furthermore, this is my house, and only I can say whether you can stay or go—not your mother. I'm telling you right now that you have to be out by the end of the year."

"What if I can't get a place before the end of the year?" Dillon snidely asked.

"Then you go move in with your mother."

Dillon rolled his eyes and said, "I can't do that. Her new boyfriend hates me."

Norman smiled and calmly said, "You reap what you sow."

Angered that his free ride was coming to an end, Dillon stormed out, repeating his earlier statement, "Like I said—you aren't my father!"

Waiting for the punctuation of the back door slamming shut, Norman said to himself, "No, if I were your father, I would have found a way to embezzle a couple of thousand dollars from you and then kicked you out of the house."

Chapter 3

The Wreck

Leaving the house for work the following morning, Norman was rather cautious as he scanned the area for Blake and especially his mother. He really didn't want to re-live his last encounter with her. He was pleased to see that the coast was clear, so he relaxed slightly as he placed his briefcase in the passenger seat and began to walk around to the driver's side of the car.

Glancing over the car before he got in, he made eye contact with Ms. Scharper, the mail delivery lady. Norman politely smiled at her, but, based on her scowl, she had not forgiven him for thinking she was still pregnant.

It seemed the number of people he was irritating was growing by the day. Ms. Scharper, Blake's mom, his ex-wife, his sister-in-law, Dillon, his brother, and his business partner. The desire to get away was building. The thought of attending the high-school reunion was more and more appealing.

His oldies radio station was saluting the year 2005. The announcer set the scene: "Eleven years ago Air France Flight 358 overran a runway at the Toronto, Canada, airport and landed in a creek, but all the passengers survived. Hurricane Katrina made landfall along the Gulf Coast, causing severe damage and killing over a thousand people and causing an estimated $108 billion in damage. The trial of Saddam Hussein began."

Kelly Clarkson's song "Breakaway" began to play.

Norman's thoughts bounced between his desire to break away from his current situation and how much happier he believed he had been 11 years earlier. In 2005, he had just gotten married and was establishing his business. Patrick was a good business partner back then and wasn't the total flake that he had grown into over the past few years. Dillon had always been a jerk, but Norman couldn't remember seeing any signs of his being a bully back then.

Once at his office, Norman walked over to Nadia's desk and asked her, "Did you ever go to your high-school reunion?"

"I went to our 10th. It was a blast! Even my husband enjoyed it. Are you going to yours? What is it—your 50th?"

With only a slight look of annoyance, he replied, "Very funny. No, it is only my 30th."

Nadia quickly sat up straight and said, "Look on the bright side; if everyone in your class aged as poorly as you have, you won't be expected to recognize anyone!"

"You need to switch to decaffeinated coffee."

She laughed before taking a more serious tone. "I think you should go. You deserve some time away from here. I think you'd enjoy it."

"Maybe you're right. Like that Kelly Clarkson song, maybe I should break away."

A minor disturbance was heard from over near Patrick's office. Both Nadia and Norman looked over in time to see a woman storm out of Patrick's office as he emerged shortly afterwards.

"Isn't that May Landy?"

Nadia agreed and added, "Her husband is Patrick's partner in that fishing boat holding company."

Norman whispered, "It would seem the client doesn't like Patrick's plans for them."

Patrick noticed Nadia and Norman watching so Patrick flashed a nervous smile and went back into his office as Ms. Landy stormed out the front door.

Norman started to go to his office when Nadia asked, "Do you have a minute that we can talk?"

"Sure. Just let me make this one call real quick. When you see me hang up, come on in."

Unfortunately for Nadia, Norman kept getting tied up with incoming calls, and she never got the chance to talk with him. When he had to leave for his lunch appointment with Yves Binkley, he remembered that Nadia had wanted to speak with him. "I am so very sorry. We never got a chance to talk, and now I have to rush off. Can it wait until I get back?"

Nadia knew he was a busy man, and she didn't want to hold him up. "It's all good! Don't worry about it. We can talk later—no problem. Hey, don't forget your raincoat. They say it's supposed to start raining in an hour or so."

Norman flashed an appreciative smile and said, "Great. We'll talk when I get back. Shouldn't be too long."

Norman met Yves Binkley at the Snoqualmie Lodge for lunch. They had a great view overlooking the falls as they discussed the plans for expanding the ice cream business. Throughout lunch, Norman probably only glanced at the waterfalls twice. For him, the excitement was in being able to show his clients the successes they had achieved in improving their business. As for Bink's Scoops, not only were they thriving, they were now expanding into two new locations. Needless to say, both Yves and Norman were thrilled with their progress.

As the meeting ended, Yves joked, "Next time we meet, I'll save the money and find someplace without a view. I don't think you even noticed the waterfalls once."

Norman laughed and admitted, "Yes, sometimes I get carried away with work and fail to smell the roses, so to speak."

As they headed for the door, Norman noticed his brother entering. "Freddie, what are you doing here?"

Fortunately, at this point, Norman was far enough away from Yves that he didn't feel compelled to introduce him to his brother. However, it was obvious that Freddie wanted to involve himself in the business meeting even if it had ended.

"Aren't you going to introduce me to your client over there? He's the guy with the ice cream shops, right?"

Pulling him to the side, Norman asked, "Why are you here?"

Freddie tried to turn on the charm and answered, "I'm trying to understand the business by joining you in your meetings and following you around."

"How'd you even know I'd be here?"

"Oh, Patrick told me. So, now what do we do? Are we going to inspect the ice cream shops or something? A double Rocky Road cone sounds great, don't you think?"

"Look, Freddie, this isn't take your child to work with you day, and you're not my son! This is my job—my career—my livelihood—not yours!"

Freddie followed Norman to the parking lot. "Listen, I'm going to continue following you around, so you might as well include me. Don't you agree that it would be far more professional to start the meeting with me than to have me barge in on it in the middle of some big negotiations?"

"Professional? How is it professional to have a family member joining my business discussions?"

"I wouldn't be a family member; I'd be a business partner."

Norman could feel his blood pressure rising. "I'm heading back to the office. We can finish this discussion there."

"Great! I'll follow you back."

Norman felt like he had just been given a brief reprieve to organize his thoughts so he could lower the boom on Freddie once and for all. He wanted to convince him that he wasn't going to get a job with him and that he was wasting his time always hanging around. In addition, he wanted to make sure Freddie kept his pushy wife away from him and his business.

As he headed down the wet winding road from Snoqualmie Falls, Norman was thinking more about the points he wanted to emphasize with Freddie than on his driving. Suddenly, a rabbit hopped onto the edge of the road. Norman honked his horn as he steered to avoid hitting the bunny.

However, the rabbit became confused and started running around in circles that took him once again into the path of Norman's car.

Out of nowhere, a large bird of prey swooped down and grabbed the rabbit in its talons and flew up towards Norman's car. He swerved back to the right to avoid hitting the bird and lost control on the wet roadway. Sliding off the roadway and through the loose gravel shoulder, he hit a pothole that slowed him down before his car hit a tree.

The impact knocked Norman out. As he regained consciousness, he heard Freddie telling him, "Hold on, Norm. Help's on the way."

The sirens he heard in the distance slowly grew louder. As he opened his eyes, Freddie asked, "Hey, are you all right?"

Norman realized that he'd been dragged from the car and was now on the wet ground. "Shouldn't you have left me in the car?"

Realizing he screwed up, Freddie immediately began to chatter. "Oh, yeah, I guess so. On account of all that spinal trauma stuff and all. I'm sorry, I guess I wasn't thinking. Are you OK? Can you move your arms and wiggle your toes? How many fingers am I holding up? What happened?"

Norman surveyed the scene and then tried to explain. He pointed towards the road and said, "Hawk..." At that point, a wet leaf fell on his face, and he paused to wipe it off. Freddie looked where

Norman was pointing and saw a lady walking her golden retriever.

Drawing the wrong conclusion about what Norman was trying to say, Freddie immediately replied, "No, man, that's not your dog, Hawk. That's just some lookie-loo curious about what happened to you. Hawk died about seven or eight years ago! Don't you remember?"

Norman was amazed by how wrong Freddie could be about what he was trying to tell him about the hawk grabbing the rabbit. Freddie mistook Norman's facial expression to mean that Norman might have lost his memory.

Before either of them could clear up the misunderstanding, the paramedics were on the scene, pushing Freddie away so they could help Norman.

At one point, he overheard Freddie tell one of the paramedics that he suspected Norman had suffered memory loss. Every time Norman tried to tell the paramedics something to confirm his memory was fine, the medics told him to be still and to be quiet.

Since he had a sizable gash in his forehead requiring stitches and they knew he had lost consciousness, they put him on a stretcher and loaded him into the ambulance. While they secured him inside, he heard Freddie ask one of the paramedics, "How long will it be before he gets his memory back?"

Again, Norman tried to say that his memory was fine when the other paramedic said, "Norman, we need you to stay as still and as quiet as possible. OK?"

On the way to the hospital, the medic asked several routine questions. "What's your full name?"

"Norman Armstrong."

"Do you know what day it is?"

"Yes, it's Friday."

Norman winced slightly as the antiseptic that had been used on his wound pained him. The medic mistakenly thought he was reacting to the questioning, so he stopped asking questions.

He started thinking about the idea that he had suffered memory loss. Had he? Other than the time he was knocked out, he felt he could remember everything that had happened. It then occurred to him that the day was actually Thursday, not Friday as he'd said. He started to correct himself, but the two medics were discussing reports and hadn't heard him.

Eventually, Norman decided to just shut up and enjoy the ride. His thoughts wandered about the dog he had named Hawk. He was a great companion who didn't really care much for Dillon or Adrianna. Norman also thought about the expression on Freddie's face when he thought Norman had memory loss.

As the medics transferred him over to the emergency room staff, he could hear one of them tell the nurse that there was some evidence of memory loss. It was interesting to see the slight change in the way people treated him once they thought he'd lost his memory. At first, it annoyed Norman that the temporary diagnosis was based on Freddie's incorrect interpretation. But then, Norman had forgotten what day it was.

The personnel in the emergency room stitched his head wound and checked his physical reflexes, however, he didn't seem too interested in determining whether he did have any memory loss. Norman tried to offer some information on the subject, but the staff were clearly focused on other matters and just continued to ask him to not speak.

Once they had finished with him in the emergency room, they wheeled him to an area and said, "Wait here for a bit. Doctor Karius will complete your examination before you can be released."

As he waited in the hall for someone to take him to the next exam, he observed a nurse stop a lady from going past the big double doors. "I'm sorry, ma'am; you can't go past this point unless you're a family member of a patient."

His attention to this exchange between the lady and the nurse was interrupted as Freddie quickly approached, bombarding him with questions. "There you are! How are you doing? Are you in pain? Are you waiting on some type of test results? Do you need anything?"

Norman was puzzled by Freddie's sudden interest in his well-being. Perhaps he really did care for him after all. This brief thought was quickly dashed as Freddie asked, "Hey, don't you think you should assign me power of attorney over your affairs while you are out of commission?"

Trying to give a quick negative response, Norman choked on his dry mouth.

Freddie said, "You need water. I'll go find you some."

With lucky timing, the orderly arrived and announced, "Hello, Mr. Armstrong. I'll take you to see Doctor Karius now."

As Freddie returned empty-handed, he followed Norman and the orderly through the large doors. The nurse he had noticed before appeared suddenly and said, "I'm sorry, sir. You can't go past this point unless you're a family member of a patient."

Freddie pointed to Norman. "Oh, it's OK—I'm his brother."

The nurse looked at the orderly and the orderly looked at Norman. "Do you know this man?"

Summoning his best poker face, Norman calmly replied, "No, I don't know him at all."

He quickly thought that he should've said, "Yes, he's my brother, but I really don't understand him at all." This would have been more accurate, but Norman was annoyed about Freddie's fake interest in his health and wanted to get away from him.

The look on Freddie's face as the nurse escorted him past the barrier was rather revealing even though Norman wasn't quite sure what to make of it. He didn't look as if he was the butt of a joke, nor was it actually brotherly concern. It seemed more like Freddie was frustrated that something hadn't gone the way he'd planned.

After the orderly left him in an examination room, he began to think about the misconception people were having about his memory loss. He thought about the pros and cons of it all and how having actual memory loss might benefit him.

For starters, he could claim ignorance regarding several recent embarrassing events. Maybe losing his memory would allow him not only fresh starts with various situations, but also perhaps a fresh perspective on his life in general.

As for his business, it would be a fairly good time to have memory loss since he had just completed a few important projects and could sit back for a couple of weeks. He also thought that in some way it might buy him some temporary relief from his partner's hounding him to buy Too Perky Coffee and his brother's hounding him to allow him to buy into his business.

Smiling slightly, he imagined how fun it would be to see Freddie's confused look again. This had all the makings of a great prank. He only wondered if he could pull it off.

The doctor knocked as he entered. "Hello, Mr. Armstrong. I'm Doctor Dawid Karius. Here is my business card."

The doctor asked several questions about his level of pain, light sensitivity, headache, and such. He ended with, "What day of the week is it?"

"Friday." Surprised that he again answered the question incorrectly, he laughed and tried to explain. "I don't know why I keep saying it's Friday when I know it's actually Thursday. The paramedic asked me the same question and…"

The doctor quickly interrupted him. "What year?"

Norman quickly realized that this was the moment of truth. Should he go ahead with the prank or should he come clean with the doctor and kiss his shot at a brief breakaway goodbye?

Feeling pressured to answer quickly, he decided to come clean and ditch the prank idea. However, as he was telling himself to 86 the idea, he actually blurted, "Eighty-six."

Realizing he had actually said this aloud, he tried to clarify himself once more, but the doctor again interrupted him.

"That's 30 years ago!"

Norman chuckled slightly at the misunderstanding and corrected his comment. "No, I meant to say that the year is '06."

The doc started looking in Norman's eyes as he flashed his light back and forth. "I suppose that's better; that's only 10 years ago."

Norman grew concerned. He knew that it was 2016, and he was actually trying to answer the question correctly, but for some reason, it came out as if he believed it was the year 2006.

The doctor saw the concern on his face. When Norman tried to explain to the doctor what he actually knew, the doctor misinterpreted it as his efforts to come to terms with forgetting the past 10 years.

Doctor Karius quickly asked, "What do you remember about 2006?"

At this point, Norman wanted to demonstrate that he remembered very well and that there was nothing wrong with him. He recalled what he remembered from the radio station's salute to 2006 from earlier in the day. "Well, let's see, Bush junior is president, Air France crashed in Toronto on landing and all the passengers survived, and Hurricane Katrina hit New Orleans."

Satisfied that he nailed the answer, he smiled confidently.

"I'm not sure about the Air France crash, but Hurricane Katrina hit New Orleans in 2005."

Norman's confident look vanished as he tried to explain that the radio announcer must have made a mistake, but the doctor asked, "What month and date is it?"

At this point, Norman became so annoyed at the questions and the doctor's unwillingness to let him explain anything that he casually responded, "Today is September 16."

Doctor Karius replied, "Today is Thursday, August 25, 2016. It appears you have a lot of history to catch up on."

As Norman began to accept the fact that he had memory loss regardless of his desire to be forthcoming about everything, the doctor asked, "What was the last local news story you remember hearing?

Realizing pretending to be stuck 10 years in the past was going to take considerable effort, Norman calmly replied, "I don't really listen to local news, but the last song I remember hearing was "Breakaway" by Kelly Clarkson."

The doctor made some notes and then asked, "What is the last business-related event you remember?"

Trying to quickly remember a business deal from 2006 caused slight panic until it occurred to him that the doctor wouldn't know a right answer from a fabricated one. "Alfred Capps wants to sell me part of his winter sporting goods store. Listen, all of these questions are giving me a splitting headache. Can I go home now?"

The doctor gave him something for the pain and scheduled a follow-up appointment for the following week.

As the orderly pushed him towards the discharge desk, he saw his brother waiting for him.

Freddie walked over to him and quickly asked, "Do you remember me? Do you know who I am?"

Amused at Freddie's hollow concern, Norman replied, "Yes, I know who you are. According to the doctor, I've only lost the memory of the past 10 years—not my whole life. Can you take me home? I seem to have left my car in a ravine."

On the ride home, Freddie bombarded Norman with questions. "Do you remember being married?"

"Yes—to Adrianna."

"Do you remember getting divorced?"

"Really?" Norman playfully asked.

"Yeah, she was having an affair behind your back."

"Was it with the butcher from Safeway?"

"No, man, it was with a used-car salesman!"

"That's interesting. She always insisted on buying new."

Pulling into his driveway, Norman was worn out from Freddie's endless questions. While some were easy, others were more challenging to answer. Walking into the house, Norman announced he was going to rest for a while.

Chapter 4

The Deception

Waking up from his nap, Norman began to second-guess the charade he was planning. Would the benefits of feigning memory loss offset the hassle of thinking about everything 10 years in the past? Even if he only kept up the pretense for a week, he began to doubt it would ever give him an advantage.

With hunger now getting the better of him, he headed to the kitchen for a snack. Dillon's rapid entry into the kitchen briefly startled him. Seeing this reaction, Dillon said, "Oh, yeah. I guess I look different than I did 10 years ago. I'm Dillon."

Norman tried to figure out how Dillon had heard about the memory loss, but assumed Freddie had told him. Wondering if his brother was still in the house, Norman glanced over towards the den.

Dillon mistakenly assumed he was looking for Adrianna. "Mom's not here. You guys divorced a couple of years ago."

Never passing up an opportunity to work a situation to his own advantage, Dillon immediately pretended to be very friendly as he tested the whole memory loss situation. "You're still going to give me the money for the Kilo Hammers concert, right?"

It was all Norman could do to keep from laughing at the absurdity that he would finance Dillon's entertainment in any form, much less an expensive concert. Pretending to be distracted slightly while searching the drawer for a knife, he managed to present a more serious expression in response to the question. "Concert? What concert and why would I agree to pay for it?"

As smooth as a seasoned con artist, Dillon replied, "Like I said, the Kilo Hammers concert. Don't you remember? You said you were going to pay my way in appreciation for all that I do for you around here."

"You do stuff around the house for me?"

Dillon laughed as if he was amazed that Norman couldn't remember all that he had done for him. Meanwhile, Norman knew the laughter was actually the result of Dillon's thinking he was pulling the wool over his eyes.

Norman's mind raced as he tried to keep his emotions in check. He was thoroughly upset that Dillon would so blatantly lie right to his face. At the same time, he was curious to see how much Dillon would try to take advantage of him. On a grander scale, he wondered who else would attempt to benefit from his memory loss and how far they would go.

"Like what kind of stuff do you do for me? I still see you as being 11 or 12 years old, and the most I remember asking of you was to not leave your clothes in the den."

"Oh, let me tell you, I do plenty around here. I wash your car every week, I mow the yard and trim the hedges, and I take care of all your computer glitches."

Norman was awed by Dillon's Oscar-winning performance. He knew that Dillon never washed any car other than his own, an outside yard service took care of the landscaping, and if he had any computer glitches, he would take his computer into work and ask Nadia to help him fix it.

Realizing his face was probably becoming very red and difficult to keep from telegraphing his total outrage with Dillon's scam, he quickly opened the refrigerator door as if he were looking for something. Hiding momentarily behind the door and breathing the cool air helped Norman regain his control.

"Yes, it does sound like you deserve something, all right."

Of course, Norman thought Dillon deserved a quick kick in the butt. Dillon thought he had the trap ready to spring.

"Great, then, you agreed to give me $400 for the tickets."

"How much? Are these front-row tickets? That's a lot of money for a concert!"

Dillon laughed mockingly. "No, they're not for front-row seats. Prices for concerts have gone up over the last 10 years. Besides, Kilo Hammers is one of the hottest concerts on the West Coast right now."

Dillon's ridicule allowed Norman time to process the value of maintaining the memory loss charade. Would it be worth $400 to him to continue the ruse for a couple more days? He wondered.

Attempting to stall for time, Norman said, "I see. Well, let me mull it over a bit and get the money to you in a couple of days."

With the skill of a telemarketer who has a live one on the hook, Dillon quickly responded, "You promised to give me the money today since the prices go up tomorrow. If you don't have the cash, you can just give me a check. Either way, I really need to get the tickets tonight before the good seats are gone."

As Norman reluctantly wrote the check, he thought to himself, "This pretending to have memory loss stuff is very expensive!"

After Dillon ran off with the $400, Norman sat quietly and contemplated the opportunity he was going to have learning the truth about people's ethics and their willingness to deliberately take advantage of him.

So far, he'd been lucky avoiding discussions that could give him away. He needed to plan more thoroughly; he would need to remember what he should forget. To this end, he started listing the major events in his life that had occurred over the past 10 years. He then spent the rest of the evening studying the list so that he wouldn't accidentally mention something that he shouldn't be able to remember.

The next morning Estella arrived to clean house. When she saw him, she asked, "How are you feeling after your accident, Mr. Armstrong? Do you remember who I am?"

Thanks to the notes he had studied, he knew that Estella had been the housecleaner since right after he married Adrianna, so he should remember her. However, he was curious how she had already heard about the wreck. "Yes, Estella, I could never forget you. Now, how did you know about the accident?"

"Oh, yes, your brother called me last night about it. Is there a lot of damage to your car?"

He just shook his head and said, "That's a very good question. I'll have to add that to my list of things I need to do today. Since the doctor wants me to take it easy, I'll work from home today."

Estella smiled and nodded as she started to leave the room. As a thought occurred to her, she turned and asked, "Are you still going to the reunion this weekend?"

With everything else that had been going on, he'd really forgotten about it. Estella saw his expression and said, "Your high-school reunion is this weekend." She then picked up the invitation on the counter. "You've been talking about attending. I was just wondering if you are still going or not."

Taking the invitation and glancing at it briefly, he chuckled as he told her, "Yes, it might be fun being around a bunch of folks who don't know any more than I do about what I've been up to over the past 10 years."

After reviewing some files from work, Norman grew restless and decided to walk around the front yard. As he plucked a couple of weeds from the front flowerbed, he glanced down the street and saw Ms. Scharper making her way to his house. As he mentally prepared himself to keep a straight face when he met her and not show any signs of embarrassment from asking her when she was due, it occurred to him that she wasn't his mail lady 10 years ago. Now all he had to do was to pretend he didn't recognize her at all.

As he glanced again to check on her progress, he noticed Blake speaking with her and then pointing at him. He quickly looked away in an effort to appear inconspicuous.

After a couple of minutes, she walked up to Norman and said hello as she handed him his mail.

"Hello. Where's George? Did he finally take his family camping over in the Olympics?"

She was momentarily confused. "George? Oh, yes, George. I replaced George on this route a couple of years ago."

Norman was relieved that now, any facial expression of embarrassment that he might show would seem to be the result of not remembering that George was no longer his letter carrier. "Oh, I see." Pointing to his bruised forehead, he added, "Ever since I bumped my head…"

"It looks like a nasty bump. Does it hurt?"

While she was very pleasant, her slight smile as she asked about his pain gave him the impression that she was secretly wishing that he was in at least minor suffering as retribution for indirectly calling her overweight.

"Yes, it's still sore. However, I find it more frustrating trying to remember things correctly. Please forgive me for forgetting your name…"

"My name is Hattie Scharper."

Wanting to shake hands, he extended his hand, but she shoved a couple of pieces of junk mail into it. "Don't worry about your memory—some things should be forgotten!"

After brief contemplation, Norman replied, "I suppose that may be true."

After she left to continue on her route, he glanced through the day's mail. He was startled by Blake's sudden voice. "Hello, Mr. Armstrong. How are you today?"

Norman almost slipped up and called him by his name, but he quickly caught himself. "Geez! You scared me! Do you make a habit of sneaking up on people? You obviously know my name. Do I know you?"

"I'm Blake. I live over in the brown house. So, Mr. Armstrong, do you want to buy some candy? It's for a good cause."

Norman could see that these were the same candy bars that had melted. He was rather disappointed to learn that even Blake was not beyond trying to take advantage of his alleged memory loss.

Picking up one of the candy bars, Norman found they were now as hard as a rock. Apparently, Blake froze all the candy to compensate for the melting. Reluctantly, Norman agreed to buy one without argument as a cheap means of maintaining his ruse.

"You get two for five dollars."

"Very well. I'll take two then."

As Blake reached in to grab two candy bars, he hesitated and then told Norman, "You know that these are the ones that melted the other day, right?"

Norman was shocked by Blake's confession as he replied, "What do you mean by melted?"

Blake started to walk away as he said, "Never mind, Mr. Armstrong. I shouldn't trick you into buying this candy."

Norman quickly stopped Blake's retreat. Quickly counting the rest of the candy bars in the box, he shoved a handful of money towards Blake. "Here, this should cover it.'

Stunned, Blake tried to ask why, but Norman just smiled and said, "I love once-melted candy."

"Wow, Mr. Armstrong—this is great! My mom promised me that if I sold all of the candy by tonight that she'd buy me a ticket to the Kilo Hammers concert."

"Is that right? Well, I'm happy for you. Tell me, how much is a ticket to the concert?"

"Twenty-five dollars."

Norman was stunned at the price difference between Blake's ticket and Dillon's, and exclaimed, "Twenty-five dollars?"

"Yeah. My mom says it's up in the nose-bleed section. Wherever that is."

Returning to the kitchen with his candy bars, Norman heard a commotion from the back yard. Upon closer investigation, he saw Estella telling the neighbor, "Go away. Mr. Armstrong is not well. Leave him alone! He needs his rest. Do you understand?"

Bernardo tried to reason with her. "I must speak to him about the property line. I need to get his signature...."

Estella was defiantly guarding her employer. "No—not today! He's not well. He has amnesia from his car wreck yesterday. He doesn't want to deal with your silliness. You go back home now."

After closing the door firmly in Bernardo's face, Estella turned to see Norman standing there listening. She was visibly embarrassed by her unprofessional conduct, but Norman smiled and said, "Thank you for that. I don't know how you knew that I didn't want to see him, but you're right. I appreciate you trying to look out for me."

As she continued with her chores, he wanted to ask when her mother was going to arrive, but realized that he couldn't since he wasn't supposed to remember anything about it. He tried to make polite conversation in hopes of learning about her mother's agenda. "What are your plans for the weekend?"

Estella smiled and replied, "Nothing as fun as you and your high-school reunion. Are you leaving tonight or in the morning to go over?"

"Oh, the reunion. Yes, well, I'll probably head over in the morning. You and your husband have big plans for next week?

Estella continued with her dusting as she said, "No vacations. We both have to work."

There still was no mention of her mother coming to stay. Norman thought that maybe she had changed her plans. Maybe she postponed her trip for some reason, or maybe she wasn't coming at all. As he struggled to come up with a creative way to find out about her mother's plans, the phone rang.

"Mr. Armstrong's residence, hello." Estella professionally greeted the caller. Norman then heard Estella say, "He's not here...No, I don't know where he is—he doesn't tell me, and I don't ask."

As she hung up, Norman said, "I'm surprised that Dillon got up and out so early this morning."

"No, sir. Dillon is still sleeping."

Seeing Norman's puzzled look, Estella clarified. "That was your ex-wife. I know you don't want to talk to her, so I keep telling her that you are not here."

After a small chuckle, he started to reply, but Estella interrupted. "You need to rest and get better. You shouldn't deal with all of these other people who give you so much stress. It's not good for you."

He thanked her for running interference for him as he realized that this was probably why her mom wasn't coming to stay. He continued to think of a clever way to bring up the topic as she carried on with her cleaning.

At lunchtime, he meandered into the kitchen to find Estella had fixed him a bowl of soup and a sandwich. "Estella, you shouldn't have! I really appreciate your thoughtfulness. Thank you."

She shrugged off the compliment as she continued to clean.

He was savoring his lunch when Dillon staggered in and asked Norman where he got the food.

Before he could answer, Estella interjected, "I made the food for him, and there is no more. If you're hungry, you can go get fast food."

Norman fought back the intense urge to burst out laughing as he continued slurping his soup.

Dillon briefly looked in the pantry and then the refrigerator for something quick to eat. Frustrated at not finding anything, he turned and looked at Norman.

Antagonistically, Norman continued to slurp his soup less quietly than usual.

Dillon blurted, "I hope there's more food in the house when Estella's mom moves in with us!"

Now Norman had his opening. "What do you mean? What is this about Estella's mom coming to stay?"

Estella, angry that Dillon mentioned it. responded. "Yes, my mother is moving here and needed a place to stay for a couple of weeks, but I've made other arrangements. It's fine."

Norman asked, "Arrangements? What arrangements? Did I already agree to have your mother stay here for some period of time?"

Estella nervously replied, "Yes, sir. You agreed she could stay here, but that was..."

"Then it's settled! She's staying here as agreed. Now, when is she arriving?"

Again, she tried to protest, but Norman wasn't hearing any of it. "Is she staying in the back room, or is Dillon moving out so she can take his room?"

As she laughed at the thought of Dillon moving out, she finally accepted Norman's offer and discussed some of the details.

Now dressed to leave, Dillon came back to the kitchen and abruptly asked, "So, do you have the $400 for my concert tickets?"

Shocked at his brazenness, Norman immediately replied, "What? I gave that to you last night!"

"Oh, you remember that, do you?"

"The doctor says my memory loss is for the 10 years before the crash—not last night."

"Oh, just thought I'd try, you know? Anyway, how 'bout giving me $20 for lunch."

Leaning back in his chair, Norman took a good look at Dillon and said, "Tell me about yourself."

Dillon just stood there, confused.

Norman tried to clarify his question. "Help me understand what happened over the past 10 years. What have you been doing since you were 12? You were always smart in school, so I guess you graduated. Did you go to college? What was your major? Did you graduate from college yet? You know, stuff like that. What are your goals and aspirations in life? What do you want to do?"

Dillon became uncomfortable with the questioning and tried to evade responding. When he tried to change the subject back to getting money for lunch, Norman interrupted him. "With the holidays coming up, have you thought about a job in retail? I'm sure they'll be hiring over at the mall, don't you think?"

Dillon snapped. "What? Work in retail? They only make minimum wage—no one can live on minimum wage!"

Norman calmly asked, "Oh? How much are you earning now?"

Dillon became furious. "You talk to me like you're my father, or something! Well, you're not my father!"

The argument increased in intensity as Dillon proceeded to yell and belittle Norman. Estella tried to intervene, asking Dillon to calm down since Norman needed to rest.

Now annoyed at her interference, Dillon yelled out, "The end of the year can't come soon enough for me!"

Pretending not to remember the ultimatum he had given Dillon, he asked, "Oh? What happens at the end of the year?"

Quickly thinking Norman forgot about telling him he had to leave by New Year's Day, he yelled back, "Just forget about it!" He then turned and stormed out.

Estella inquired, "Did you order Dillon out of the house before January?"

In a low mumble, he replied, "The way he acts, I'm surprised I gave him that long to get out."

Smiling with approval, she twinkled as she said, "Maybe he'll be motivated to leave before the year's end."

Norman smiled and said, "Well, at least he left before I gave him $20 for lunch!"

Chapter 5

The Reunion

Early the next morning, Norman began driving towards Ellensburg for his reunion. The traffic was light, and the sun was shining brightly as he drove through the Cascade Mountains. He found it very relaxing as his mind began to remember growing up in central Washington state. Each curve in the road brought back different memories and experiences.

Crossing a small creek, he thought back to when he took a date up the trail on the right so they could watch an osprey in the moonlight. As he stopped in the small town of Cle Elum for breakfast, he remembered the handful of gigs his small band had played in the local taverns. Later, when he passed the fruit stand in Thorpe, his mouth watered for his mother's delicious fruit desserts and pies.

He hadn't been back to Ellensburg since he left for college. However, the town hadn't changed too drastically in the interim. The major interchanges were still there as were the fairgrounds and billboards advertising the upcoming Labor Day rodeo. He drove past his childhood home and noted the decorative changes the new occupants had made.

Stopping briefly at a small coffee shop, he tried to get a handle on his feelings. He had several good memories of growing up in this town, yet he was now an outsider, a stranger who hadn't kept in touch with his friends. How would his friends greet him? Would they look down upon him for having abandoned them all? He quickly realized that it wasn't too late to just leave and go back home. Still, he was curious. Whatever became of his friends?

After a last gulp of coffee, he summoned his strength to head over to the school gymnasium for the first of the weekend's activities for the class of 1986. After all, he thought, he'd given high-stakes presentations to leaders of industry—how difficult would facing some former classmates be?

Even though he was a few minutes late, the parking lot wasn't very full. The few people he saw walking into the gym were not familiar. He laughed slightly to himself as he considered the possibility that he was invited to the wrong reunion. This notion quickly passed as he saw a big banner on the back wall for the class of '86.

Between 30 years of aging and the high number of spouses, Norman was having difficulty recognizing anyone. He even briefly considered the possibility that he really had lost his memory.

His fears started to vanish when he recognized a couple of people across the room. Naturally, these other folks were whispering among themselves as they indiscreetly pointed towards Norman. Just as he was about to ponder the idea that he might have changed greatly over the years and be unrecognizable to others, he heard a loud voice from a different direction.

"Norman Armstrong! It is you, right?"

Being recognized by anyone made Norman happy, but seeing that it was his old friend Walter Polk put a big smile on his face.

"Walt! How are you? I was beginning to wonder if I was going to know anyone here today."

The two laughed and re-told several stories of past shenanigans. When Norman asked, "Walt, what do you do these days to pay the bills?"

Walt quickly looked around and then quietly replied, "I do a lot of computer stuff. You know, like cyber security and data protection."

"I always remember you as kind of a conspiracy theorist. Did you get into this line of work trying to keep Uncle Sam's eyes out of your personal business?"

Stepping closer and lowering his voice, Walt answered. "Hey, just because you're paranoid doesn't mean that they aren't out to get you! Anyway, I found that I have a gift for getting into secured computers. I just go around now and try to fix computers so I can't get in anymore."

"So, you're a hacker?"

"Hey, not so loud! I prefer to call it research. The more ways I find to get into your computer just provides me with more information on how I can prevent others from doing the same."

Before Norman could ask a follow-up question, he was interrupted.

"I saw Walt here last week at the Eagles meeting, but Norman, I don't think I've seen you in 20 years!"

"Emit Feaster! How are you doing? I see you still have all of your hair—why haven't you gone bald like the rest of us?"

"Good genes and good living, I suppose! Tell me, where are you at now? Last I remember you were working down in Colorado, weren't you?"

Norman remembered that he and Emit had both gone into business out of college and kept in loose contact with each other for a couple of years until they lost track of each other. "I'm over in the Puget Sound area. Still buying, re-tooling, and selling businesses for a buck here and a couple of bucks there. Where are you at these days, Emit? You still own that chain of small independent hotels?"

Emit stood proud and proclaimed, "Yes! I now have 23 hotels across Washington, Oregon, Idaho, and Montana. You know how it is, though; some days you're the wolf, and some days you're the rabbit."

After a few shared stories, Emit remembered something. "Hey, Norman, didn't you have something to do with Solhugtok Labs?"

Norman was surprised that Emit knew anything about the small tech company. "Yes, I worked with them several years ago until they got really secure and bought me out. Last I heard they were doing fairly well for themselves."

Emit exclaimed, "That's an understatement! I don't know if you have any stock in their company, but if you do—hold on to it! I hear they just developed some gadget that will revolutionize the solar energy industry making solar power extremely affordable to the average homeowner."

Norman didn't have the heart to tell Emit that he had given all of his shares in Solhugtok Labs to his wife in their divorce. He just asked, "So you think it's going to be worth something, do you?"

"I'm telling you, Norman, their stock value will take off at a pace unseen since Starbucks or Amazon!"

Norman smiled as he replied, "I remember my business partners from there very well, and I am sincerely very happy for them. I hope this gizmo you mentioned is very successful for them. They truly deserve it."

The alumni turnout at the gym was light. Either people were not interested in participating in the reunion, or they were holding off to attend the dinner that evening. Walt, Emit, and Norman went to a local tavern and continued their walk down memory lane.

After a couple of beers and a few dozen laughs, the three high-school friends were once again as comfortable with one another as they had been in their senior year. Norman especially enjoyed being able to let his guard down. He didn't have to pretend he didn't remember some event or worry about saying the wrong thing. While the others bared their lives to one another, Norman brought them up to date about his troublesome brother, obnoxious business partner, pushy neighbor, and his bullying stepson.

The solutions they offered for each of their problems ranged from poignant to absurd and from serious to hilarious and occasionally illegal.

Reflecting back on his list of woes that he had unveiled to his friends, Norman said, "Thinking about all of this really makes me feel like a loser. I'm glad you both are getting such a kick out of it all."

As their chuckles subsided, Emit calmly added, "Norm, you're not too old to start over, you know? I dare say this area could benefit from someone with your skills. You could start a new business with no partners or at least with a partner you can work with and trust."

With a smile, Norman said, "I have to say, starting over here sounds very appealing."

"Before you leave town, you may want to take a look at the farm supply store out on the Kittitas Highway. You could really make some improvements there and get your foot in the market over here."

While Norman was thinking about the prospects and opportunity, Walter chimed in. "Hey, I just realized that I know a surveyor who could answer your concerns about your property line back home. My old college roommate is a surveyor over in Renton—I'm sure he could help you out. He can be there anytime you need."

With a suspicious look, Norman asked, "How can he be any good at his job if you don't even need an appointment to see him?"

Walter laughed as he answered, "Don't worry about it! He owes me a big favor. For me—he'll drop everything to be at your place."

Seeing Norman and Emit exchange inquisitive glances, Walter explained. "His name is Armadillo Bue, but everybody calls him Arm. One day, I was doing some computer... uh..., well, let's just say I was doing some computer research. Anyway, I sort of got into Arm's computer and remotely turned on his screen camera. How was I to know I'd find him dancing and singing in his underwear to a Justin Bieber song? Anyway, I may have led him to believe that I recorded the event. I promised him that I wouldn't post it on the Internet as long as he did favors for me from time to time."

Astonished, Emit slowly asked, "How is that even remotely legal?"

Anticipating Walter's response, Norman was able to simultaneously reply with him, "It's complicated!"

Walter quickly looked at his watch and announced, "Wow, look at the time! We've got to get going if we're going to the reunion dinner."

The drive over to the armory building didn't take long. As they walked from the parking area to the reunion, they began to see a few familiar faces. Norman felt fortunate to have Emit and Walter coaching him on everyone's names as well as their current situations.

Once inside, the three drifted off in separate directions. Norman got a bottle of water at the refreshment table. As he took a sip, he noticed Leila across the room. He caught himself staring at her. Seeing her again took his breath away momentarily. As soon as he composed himself, he strolled casually over towards her. As he approached her, it was as if she had some type of radar going because she turned towards him, smiled, and said, "I wondered how long it would take you to say hello.'

He laughed as he stammered a response. "If you knew I was here, why didn't you come over and say hello to me?"

Shaking her head with a disappointed smirk, she replied, "Oh, Norman, still wanting the ladies to make the first move?"

Perplexed, Norman stammered as he tried to produce a clever reply. However, Leila took pity on him and rescued him. "How are you, Norm? It's been far too long since I last saw you."

They just stood there for a moment looking at one another before Norman said, "You look wonderful, Leila. The years have been very nice to you. Do you still sing?"

With a modest smile, she replied, "Yes, I still sing with various groups from time to time. I even get called on to fill in for touring back-up singers who have to bail out due to poor health and such. What about you? Do you still play the bass guitar?"

With a regretful expression, he said, "I haven't played publicly in years. Just too busy, I guess. I do sort of miss it, or maybe I just miss being in a band with you."

Leila scoffed, "I swear, Mr. Armstrong, I do believe you are flirting with me."

The two of them began to make the rounds, stopping to chat frequently with other alumni. He told her about his marriage and divorce, and she told him that she was single and working in marketing. As soon as the two of them started to relax with one another, a former classmate asked if they were married to one another. After the third such encounter, he suggested, "You know, we should just tell them that we are married and see their reaction."

"Oh, heavens, no! News like that would spread like wildfire in a little town like this. It'd be fine for you living across the mountains, but I have to live here!" She paused briefly before flashing him a mischievous grin. "Besides, if that's your way of proposing to a girl, well, I'll just hold out for something a little more elaborate."

Walter briskly walked over to them and said, "Hey, Norman, did Leila tell you how I helped her with a little problem she was having?"

As Norman shook his head, Leila tried to explain. "You remember Chad, don't you? Well, for some reason he got fixated on me and wanted me to go out with him. He just wouldn't take no for an answer. Eventually, he started stalking me everywhere I went."

Walter was too excited not to interrupt. "Like Leila said, he was stalking her. So, I got busy, uh you know, researching Chad's computer. Anyway, I found several messages between him and some friend of his up in Canada."

Leila decided to interrupt Walter this time. Giggling, she added, "Those notes showed Chad bad-mouthing everyone from family to co-workers and trashing his so-called close friends and even his boss."

Walter, with a sly wink, then said, "Somehow, all these notes got posted to social media with all of his victims tagged so that they could see how he really felt about them. Strange how that could have happened.”

Norman asked with a straight face, “So, I take it Chad will not be coming to the reunion?”

“Lord no! He packed up and left town. No one’s heard from him since.” As she gave Walter a sly smile, she added, “If I knew who was responsible for posting those notes online, I’d thank them.”

“I don’t think anyone will ever know how that happened,” Walter laughed.

Norman inserted, “You better hope not!”

Walter then looked at Leila and asked, “Hey, did you hear that Emit is trying to talk Norman here into moving back to town?”

Norman quickly tried to change the subject by calling out to some alumni whom he had not greeted yet. As Walter slipped away into the crowd, Leila just stared at Norman with her classic “Is that so?” expression.

As the evening wound down, Emit suggested that Walter, Norman, and Leila meet him for lunch at the local diner. After agreeing, they parted ways, and Norman asked if he could take Leila home.

The two of them talked for hours about what they had been doing for the past 30 years. They found it interesting that as much as they had changed, the comfort they had with one another was still the same.

“Are you really thinking about moving back here?”

“I don’t know. It’s a big decision to terminate your life in one spot, pull up your roots, move someplace new, and try to start all over again.” Norman snickered softly. “I suppose it sounds worse than it really would be. You see, I really don’t have any roots there. At least, not like Walter, Emit, and you have here. The truth is, I guess I’m just scared.”

Leila took Norman's hand and asked, "Are you scared to find out there is nothing keeping you there or are you fearful of plunging into the unknown?"

They sat in silence for a bit before Norman got up the nerve to lean towards Leila for a kiss. She turned towards him and began to close her eyes when the car lit up from the headlights of a car, effectively destroying the mood. Norman asked, "Do you ever go to the lookout we used to go to in high school?"

"A couple of times I've driven up to see the changing colors of the seasons. It was always during the day, and I never took anyone with me."

He immediately started the car and headed towards their spot. The sky was getting bright as dawn was approaching. Leila had to help him with the directions since a few of the familiar landmarks had changed. By the time they reached the crest of the range, the sun had already appeared on the horizon.

Once they arrived at their spot, they strolled over to a large boulder that they had sat on together many times before. They laughed and talked about all sorts of things. During one of the rare periods of silence between them, Leila pointed and said, "Look at the shadow of the tree over there. The sun has dried the dew all around except in the shadows."

Norman added, "The dew is so white it looks like frost."

There was something about this that made him get serious for a moment. She noticed and rested her hand on his shoulder as she asked, "Are you OK?"

"Back home I've been living a lie for a couple of days now. It started as a prank but somehow spiraled out of control. Anyway, folks there think I have memory loss and can't remember anything that's happened to me in the past 10 years."

She started to ask him to explain, but he continued before she could. "It's really been an eyeopener for me. People will lie right to my face as brazen as can be when they think I don't know any better. I guess I never really knew how quickly some folks would jump at the chance to deceive me."

Leila pointed towards the tree shadow and said, "It sounds like it's a lot like frost in the shadows, or in this case, dew. It's there, lurking in the shadows, and you can't see it until you get a chance to look at it from a fresh perspective."

Norman looked at the glistening dew and then told Leila, "You can't un-see it. You know it was there, and you know it'll be there again in the morning. I want to shine a light on it and dry it up once and for all."

"Sounds a lot like you are plotting revenge."

"No, not revenge. I just want some measure of justice with a good dose of karma."

After they laughed, Leila asked, "I had no idea you felt that everyone was trying to take advantage of you."

"There are folks who have really changed my opinions about them in a positive direction through all of this. The neighbor kid, Blake, and my housekeeper, Estella, and even my assistant at work, Nadia, have all sprung to my defense and tried to help me. So, I've been able to see the good in some folks too."

Realizing they needed to get a couple hours of sleep before they met the others for lunch, they decided it was time to head back to town. While walking her back to the car, Norman stopped and said, "I don't think we ever came here when I didn't kiss you!"

Leila chuckled as she replied, "Well, there's a first time for everything."

He laughed softly as they continued towards the car. As he reached to open her door for her, she said, "Of course, this doesn't have to be that time."

The kiss that followed was a message in and of itself. It said more to one another than their previous hours of conversation.

"Well, Mr. Armstrong, you still know how to curl a girl's toes."

"I don't know how it's possible, but your lips are as beautiful as they were back in high school."

As they got into the car, Leila playfully answered, "I do lip exercises daily." She then began to make several faces with her lips in extreme positions and shapes. "Sure, I know it looks funny, but I guess you're happy with the results."

After a few hours of rest, Norman met the others at the diner. Emit and Walter were laughing about something as he approached their table. Seeing Norman, Walter stood and got serious as he asked him, "Who is May Landy? By chance is she your business partner's girlfriend?"

"Who? May Landy? Oh, yes, I believe she is the wife of one of Patrick's clients. How did you get her name?"

Walter saw someone getting ready to leave the diner he needed to speak to. With a quick grin, Walter just replied, "I'll be back."

Emit interjected, "Did you say one of Patrick's clients? Wouldn't that make them one of your clients too?"

As Norman sat down at the table, he tried to explain. "Our clients are either his, mine, or ours, depending on the original arrangement with them."

Emit tilted his head as he asked, "Then what prevents you from taking clients over here on your own and then weaning yourself away from your involvement with your partner?"

Before Norman could respond, Emit added, "I spoke this morning with the owner of that farm supply store I told you about. He's interested in talking to you about how you could help them."

"Great! You already have a client over here." Leila exclaimed as she walked up to the table unnoticed. "Sorry I'm late, guys. I didn't get much rest last night."

Emit wasn't surprised to see his friends getting along so well. He always thought they were perfect for each other and had never understood why they never married.

Norman was steadfastly keeping his enthusiasm in check as he discussed a couple of perceived obstacles to his moving back to

central Washington. This caused his friends to smile since they knew it meant he was seriously contemplating the transition.

As Walter returned to the table, he overheard some remark about Norman setting up an office. "That's great news! I can be your IT guy. I'll have business cards printed up with my title—Computer Czar."

As Leila laughed, Emit urged her not to encourage him. Norman calmly said, "Listen, I sincerely appreciate your collective encouragement with this concept. I really do. It's just that there is a lot to consider."

Emit leaned forward as he spoke. "I don't mean to be insensitive here, but you have toxic relationships with your partner, brother, and sister-in-law. You need to step away from that environment. What better place to come to than here?"

Walter dryly added, "It took you 30 years to get back here—my guess is it'll take a lot longer for those guys to find their way over here."

Leila interjected, "You need to get away from your neighbor too. Think about it; selling your house is one sure way to get your deadbeat stepson to finally move out."

After taking turns pointing out some of the advantages to moving back, they sat quietly to allow Norman a chance to digest it all and respond. "As liberating as it all sounds to me, I don't think I can get past the feeling that I'd be running away. More importantly, I'd always feel like I let them all get away with taking advantage of me."

Leila looked at Walter and Emit, and added, "Norman wants to stay long enough to witness karma."

"Well, if you want karma, I can help that along!" Walter gleefully offered as Emit gave him a suspicious glance.

Wanting to dampen their exploding enthusiasm, Norman calmed them down and said, "Listen, I don't wish harm on anyone. I just think some of these people need to be taught an important life lesson that you shouldn't take advantage of people just because you think you can get away with it."

Leila and Emit grew contemplative as Walter asked with a puzzled expression, "Does this mean you will not need my friend Arm to survey your property?"

"I really could use Arm's help settling the dispute with my neighbor. Thank you."

Emit handed Norman a piece of paper with his handwritten notes. "I made a list of some steps you may want to discuss with your lawyer if you decide you want to dissolve the partnership. I'm sure there's nothing you aren't already aware of, but I just thought it would make a useful reminder for you."

"Thanks, Emit. My lawyer is certainly on my side since I knew him long before my dealings with Patrick."

After some farewell wishes, Emit left while the remaining three randomly discussed various options. Walter appeared to have had an epiphany when he blurted, "Does your business partner ever sleep in his office?" Without waiting for a reply, he continued, "If he does, I have some old bear traps that we can place on the floor near him so when he wakes up he'll step...."

"Stop right there! Hold on a minute. What part of not wanting to physically hurt anyone did you not understand?"

Walter countered, "Oh, Norm, the sharp edges have all been filed down. It wouldn't sever anything."

Leila added, "It'd leave a nasty bruise."

"No bear traps! No physical or property damage, and no breaking the law! Understood?"

Walter started to ask, "When you say breaking the law..." but Leila stopped him before he could finish his request for clarification.

After Norman gave them both a stern look, they both reluctantly agreed to his stipulations.

The three friends talked and laughed about a wide range of topics for the next few hours. Realizing Norman would be heading back home before nightfall, Leila started casually encouraging Walter to leave so she could be alone with Norman. Unfortunately, Walter didn't take subtle hints well.

"Walter, didn't you say you had a bunch of stuff to do at home before going to work early tomorrow?"

"Oh, don't worry about me. I took tomorrow off thinking Norman might hang around an extra day."

"I thought you were going to help your nephew with his school project since it had to do with computers."

"Yeah, I was going to, but my sister-in-law insists that he do it all on his own."

Norman chimed in, "That's very commendable of you to offer and of your sister-in-law for holding him accountable. It's important to take responsibility for your own work."

Eventually, Leila gave up trying to be subtle and just said, "Walter, I want you to leave now so I can have Norman to myself for a while before he leaves to go home."

Walter quickly glanced at Norman who was shocked. Walter looked at her and asked, "Is this why you keep kicking me in the shin?"

Leila smiled but didn't respond.

"Okay! You win—I'm out of here." Walter then left promising to keep in touch with Norman about ways to give karma a helping hand.

Norman smiled as he asked her, "Do you always get your way?"

With a sly smile, she just replied, "Not yet." Then, with a feigned look of shock, she asked, "Why? Would you have rather Walter stayed? I can call him back if you want."

Norman tilted his head as he said, "You make the concept of moving back here seem so irresistible. I don't seem to have a problem keeping Walter and Emit grounded with their ideas about me moving back here. But you—I have a difficult time saying no to you."

The two talked, laughed, and flirted with one another for another hour before Norman reluctantly announced he had to leave. He asked for her number, but she refused. "No, sir, Mr. Armstrong! I'm not falling for that old trick. It might be another 30 years before I hear from you. Why don't you give me your number, this time?"

After they exchanged their contact information, Leila started to make some funny remark, but Norman placed his hands on her cheeks and pulled her close for a meaningful kiss. They were quiet as they cherished the rush of blood through their veins.

With a slight smirk, she said, "Indeed! You are still a toe-curling kisser."

Crossing the Cascades as he made his way home, Norman reflected on his fun-filled weekend. He realized that he was happier than he'd been in a long time. His reunion showed him several elements that had been missing from his life, such as good friends and the special connection he shared with Leila. He thought about her all the way home. He was certain that it would not take another 30 years to get back in touch with her.

Chapter 6

Washing the Rental

As Norman finished breakfast, he heard a knock on the door. Quickly reminding himself that people still believed he was experiencing memory loss, he focused himself before answering the door. Seeing it was his ex-wife, he quickly looked at his watch to signal her that he didn't have time for her unexpected visit.

"Good, your gatekeepers aren't around to prevent my visit this time!"

"Gatekeepers?"

"Your housekeeper, Estella, and that lady in your office, Nadia. They are always blocking my calls saying that you're too busy. Whatever!"

She barged her way in as she glanced around to see if anyone was around to hear them talking.

Norman sarcastically said, "Adrianna, what a pleasant surprise. Won't you come in? I'd call you by your new last name, but I don't know what it is." He knew that she had kept his name since she had never remarried but was trying to annoy her about it.

She gave him an unamused glare.

He then said, "I understand we divorced. I can't imagine why."

Rolling her eyes, she replied, "When you are done with your little comedy routine, we need to talk."

"Oh, great! You came to get Dillon and his things, and finally move him out of here?"

Trying not to let his remarks upset her, she just quickly replied, "No, besides, you gave him until the end of the year."

Norman threw on his best surprised look and said, "Oh? I guess that's part of my memory I'd forgotten. Thanks for reminding me."

She was now angry at herself for volunteering info about Dillon, but she continued to focus on the primary reason for her visit. "Yes, well, about this whole memory loss thing, I hope you haven't forgotten about deciding to give me the *Marian Rose*."

Norman knew that he had never agreed to give her the boat. However, he also remembered how expensive it would be, thanks to Dillon, to get it seaworthy again. Stalling for a little more time to plan his strategy for dealing with this deception, he just asked, "The *Marian Rose*?"

"Yes, the *Marian Rose*. The boat we got right after we were married. You know how much I loved that boat. So, you agreed to give it to me."

With a straight face, he replied, "I was just going to give you the boat? Besides, if you loved it so much, why wasn't it part of the division of property when we divorced?"

Trying to be charming, she softened her tone as she explained. "Oh, Norm, don't you remember? We didn't want to complicate the divorce any more than necessary, so we decided that you would sign the boat over to me afterwards."

"What was I supposed to get in exchange?"

Playing coy, she said, "Well, at the time, you mentioned that you really wanted the 2,000 shares of some laboratory stock you were forced to give me in the divorce. My accountant says it could be really valuable in a few years. I suppose that, if you insisted, I could trade you the stock for the boat."

Norman could not believe his luck. He knew he had to keep his best poker face since he didn't want to appear too eager or reveal the flaws of the deal for Adrianna. He knew her well enough to know that if anyone had suggested the value of the stock would increase anytime in her lifetime, she wouldn't have offered it for trade.

Intentionally, he knocked some magazines off a table as a distraction so he could focus more clearly on the proposed deal. As an explanation, he told her, "Ever since the accident, it appears I have lost some of my coordination along with my memory. Now, what stock are you talking about—a laboratory of some type?"

Pulling a folder out of her purse, she said, "I brought it along with me, just in case. It's Slough-Track or something like that. For some reason, you thought the stock was special and didn't want to part with it. So, here's your chance to get it back. If you have the title to the boat, we can each sign the documents and be on our way."

Wondering if he could obtain anything else in this deal, Norman quickly entered Solhugtok Labs into the computer to find the current stock price. Seeing that it was only trading at a fraction above 50 cents per share, he asked, "Don't you think the boat is worth more than a thousand dollars?"

Adrianna smiled slightly, giving away the secret that she had planned for this step in the negotiation. "Do you remember that Larry Pirnie painting we got that time over in Missoula?"

Norman's mind raced as he tried to remember if he was supposed to be able to remember this event or not. Furthermore, he was confused by the question since the painting, the last he saw, was hanging in his dining room. He stammered a partial response. "Painting from Missoula?"

"Yes, it's a limited edition print by Larry Pirnie. You always said how much you loved it because of the bright colors. Don't you remember?"

He wanted to answer her that he did know the painting and that it was hanging in the other room, but he was too curious to find out where she was going with this subject. His look of uncertainty caused her to elaborate. "Well, you gave that to me a while back, and I have to tell you that I was going to list it on the Internet for sale. I have it in the car now since I wanted Dillon to help me take a couple of good pictures of it for the online advertisement. If you still like it, maybe I could add that to the deal."

Norman was so angry he was about to scream. The only thing that he could figure was that Dillon must have taken the picture off the wall and given it to his mother. Now, she was trying to sell it back to him as if no wrongdoing had occurred. Any minor feeling of guilt over trading away a boat that required over $5,000 in repairs had now vanished.

Pretending to ponder the idea momentarily, he eventually agreed. "Go get the painting, and I'll get the title to the boat. You have yourself a deal."

Within a couple of minutes, he had his painting and stock back, and she had the title and keys to a boat in need of heavy repairs. Before she left, he said, "Now, about Dillon..."

Immediately she began to whine. "Oh Norm, you know this is much closer to all his friends. He's very comfortable here. Besides, it really wouldn't be fair to my new boyfriend since Dillon isn't his son."

"Dillon's not my son either! He's your son. More importantly, he is in his twenties and should be living on his own somewhere paid for from his own salary."

Adrianna turned to walk towards the door. "I really don't have time to get into this now. Maybe in a week or two. I'll try to get back with you about it."

Exasperated, Norman said, "Well, can you at least pay me back for the $400 I just gave him for the Kilo Hammers concert he wants to go to?"

She started laughing as she headed towards her car. Over her shoulder, she hollered back at Norman. "No way! I already gave him $300 for the same ticket a week ago."

As soon as she drove off, he ran to the dining room to look at the wall where his painting had been on display. There he found a cheap landscape painting hanging as a replacement. He wondered how long his Pirnie had been missing. He then wondered what thrift store the replacement picture came from.

Divided between anger from having his painting stolen and then offered back to him as payment and euphoria over getting rid of his costly boat, he quietly shook his head in disbelief.

Walking into his kitchen for a cup of coffee, he heard a knock on the back door. He wanted to ignore it, but unfortunately was seen through the window. It was his neighbor Bernardo. As he walked to the door, he realized that since Bernardo had moved in within the past year, Norman shouldn't appear to recognize him.

In his friendliest voice, Norman greeted the caller. "Hello, may I help you?"

"Do you recognize me?"

Not wanting to blatantly lie, he answered, "Should I?"

With a slight smile, the neighbor replied, "I am Bernardo, and I moved in next door a few months ago. I started to build a small garage only to discover that your fence is on my property."

Looking past Bernardo over towards the fence, he pretended to be surprised, "Oh, really? I wonder how that could've happened."

"No matter how it happened, it needs to be moved at least five feet back towards your house. You agreed to move it just a couple of weeks ago. I just stopped by to see if you knew when you were going to have this done."

Knowing he never agreed to move the fence without performing his own survey, Norman started asking Bernardo several questions. "Please forgive me. They tell me I have some memory loss from my accident a few days ago. Tell me again. How did you find out that the fence is on your property line? Did you have a surveyor come out to confirm this? If so, did they put stakes along the true property line?"

Appearing a little nervous, Bernardo answered, "Oh sure, I had a surveyor mark it all off. I'm sure he put out some pins or something. Sorry about your accident and all. Listen, to help you out, why don't I get a guy to move the fence, and I can just have him send you the bill. Would that be okay with you?"

Avoiding being backed into a corner, Norman snapped his fingers and exclaimed, "Hey, now I understand! I had a message from a guy telling me that he was going to be here this week to survey my property. I didn't know why I needed that and was going to call and cancel. I guess I should have him do his thing and stake out the property line once and for all. Don't you agree?"

Bernardo shoved a document at Norman, saying, "Oh yes! That was my guy calling you. You see, when I had the line surveyed. you agreed to pay half. He was just calling for his half of the payment. This is the document showing his findings."

As Norman started to review the document from Bernardo's surveyor, the neighbor tried to distract Norman by saying, "I can have someone here to move the fence tomorrow as long as you agree to pay for it."

Norman slowly shook his head. "No, I'm pretty sure he said that I had called him to survey my property. He didn't say anything about collecting any payment for work already completed. Anyway, he should be here tomorrow and answer all of our questions."

Bernardo was visibly annoyed at this point. "It is a total waste of money to survey the same property line twice. I sincerely hope you don't expect me to pay half of a second survey!"

Norman's enjoyment at seeing his neighbor get upset caused him to grow bold enough to make a proposition. "I have an idea! If the survey confirms my fence is on your property, then I'll pay for both surveys in addition to the expense of moving my fence. However, if the fence is more than six inches on my side of the established property line, then you'll have to pay for both surveys and moving the fence. Deal?"

As the two men shook hands, Bernardo angrily asked, "What happens if the fence doesn't need to be moved?"

Stunned that Bernardo would even suggest the possibility that the fence was in the correct location, Noman smiled politely and said, "I suppose that would mean that we would each only have to pay the surveyor we hired."

Stepping farther out onto the back patio to watch his neighbor storm away, Norman heard something going on in the front of his house. As he went to investigate, he saw Blake washing his car.

Puzzled, Norman slowly walked over to Blake. "Gosh, Blake, thank you for washing my rental car, but it really isn't necessary. I mean seriously—it's a rental. What possessed you to do this?"

"Hello, Mr. Armstrong. These rims aren't very easy to get clean. Do you have any tips on how I can get these things more shiny?"

Norman mentioned a couple of ideas how Blake might be able to loosen the dirt from the wheels with less effort and how to clean the windows without streaks. Blake thanked him for the suggestions and pointed out a small leak in his garden hose. "I don't know when the leak started, but I don't think it was because of anything I did."

Norman laughed and assured him that it wasn't important. Realizing Blake still had not answered his question, he repeated it. "Blake, why are you washing my rental car?"

"Oh, man, I'm pretty sure I'm not supposed to tell you."

Norman slowly shook his head. "I don't understand. You're not supposed to tell me what?"

"Dillon promised not to pick on me if I washed his car once a week. Only, his car isn't here this morning so I figured I'd wash this car, so Dillon couldn't say I didn't fulfill my obligation for this week."

Norman became livid with Dillon and started to tell Blake to stop washing cars for him when his phone started ringing. In a rage, he answered it without first checking the caller ID. This was a big mistake since it was his sister-in-law calling.

Instantly, Brandi started listing reasons Norman should make Freddie partner. As soon as he could interject a comment, he tried to turn down the notion. "Listen, Brandi, Freddie doesn't have what it takes to…"

Brandi interrupted, "Norm, you listen! Here's the deal. Freddie is your brother. It's your job to take care of him. You got a business, and he needs a job. Give it to him!"

With a partial laugh, Norman replied, "If Freddie was still a child or even if he was in his teens, maybe, just maybe, it would be my job to take care of him since our parents are no longer around. That's not the case, is it? He's an adult, and I am not responsible for his success or failure. On the other hand, it is my company, and I am responsible for the success or failure of my business. Making him a partner would not be a successful move."

Defiantly, Brandi asked, "Really? What are you basing that opinion on?"

Thinking quickly, he realized that every example he wanted to cite had happened in the last few years. To suddenly remember these examples would expose the truth about his memory. His hesitation only encouraged Brandi to continue her rant. "At least you can put him in charge of a single account. Maybe you can put him in charge of the Too Perky Coffee chain."

He straightforwardly stated, "We are not buying that business!"

Deciding to take a different approach, she exclaimed, "If you don't give him a job, I'm going to divorce him, and it will be all your fault!"

Norman fully expected to hear a dial tone after her outburst, but surprisingly, she was awaiting a response. He thought that since she didn't hang up on him, maybe he should hang up on her. "I'm getting a little light-headed walking around in the yard. I think I need to go lay down now." He then ended the call.

Remembering that he was talking to Blake about washing the car, he quickly turned around to repeat his instructions that he wasn't to wash any more cars for Dillon. However, Blake had evidently finished the task and had gone back home.

The more he thought about the excuse he had given Brandi, laying down started to sound like a great idea. So, he headed for the couch and stretched out.

After a few minutes of snoozing, he was jolted awake when Dillon barged into the room. "What's the matter, old man—you need your nap to get through the day?"

Not yet awake enough to formulate a witty response, Norman mumbled, "I guess I'd have to nap quite a bit to compete with the amount of sleep you accumulate not getting up until after noon every day."

"Whatever! So, you decided to stay home because of a little bump on the head? Sheesh, what a lightweight! Hey, since you took the day off, maybe you can go grocery shopping—we need a bunch of stuff."

Shaking out the cobwebs from his nap, Norman stood and was primed to unload on Dillon. However, right as he got his attention, they heard someone entering the front door. Shortly afterwards they saw Estella and her mom entering the room. Estella introduced Isidora to everyone and then explained. "My mom caught an earlier flight and is a day early. I really hope it's still okay for her to stay here even though she is early."

Norman eagerly welcomed Isidora and insisted, "It's no problem arriving early."

Turning towards Dillon, they expected to get some type of similar assurance, but all they got from him was a mumbled, "Great! The circus has now arrived." He then turned and went to his room.

Norman started to scold him for his rudeness, but he had already left the room. Embarrassed, Norman faced Isidora and apologized for Dillon's behavior.

Isidora and Estella exchanged a few remarks in Spanish before Isidora smiled and extended her hand while saying, "Espero que tengas un buen dia."

Norman nervously smiled as he replied, "I'm sorry, it's been a number of years since I took Spanish in college. I'm rather rusty at it."

Estella gave her mother an annoyed glance as she asked her to speak in English.

In a heavy accent, Isidora appeared to struggle as she said, "uh, I hope, uh…what, uh…you have, uh…a, uh…good day."

Estella looked even more annoyed at her mom, but Isidora simply raised her hand and said something in Spanish to her daughter. Estella raised a brow as she slowly shook her head in apparent confusion. However, she didn't say another word as she picked up her mother's luggage and headed to the spare bedroom.

Chapter 7

Forgery

Noticing the time, Norman realized that he had a follow-up doctor's appointment regarding his alleged memory loss. On the way to the appointment, he debated the merits of telling his doctor the truth about his memory. Naturally, this led to his thinking about all of the reasons he had for continuing the charade. When he realized his chest was tightening and his grip on the steering wheel had increased, he tried to think of other more peaceful topics. He certainly didn't need to have the doctor misdiagnose him with high blood pressure too.

As soon as the doctor entered the examination room, he asked Norman, "Do you remember who I am?"

Having decided to level with the doctor, Noman started to explain. "Listen, doc, the other day when I was in here…"

Doctor Karius interrupted Norman's effort to explain. "It's quite all right if you don't remember me. It wouldn't be beyond reason that you might forget. I sense that your reluctance to answer me with a specific yes or no is somehow revealing of your possible embarrassment that you can't remember. So, please rest assured that it is OK."

"Yes! I remember you. I remember everything."

"Oh, so you got your memory back? That's great news. When did you start remembering?"

Norman took a deep breath to keep from losing his patience with the doctor. "I've always remembered. I never had any memory loss. Everybody kept assuming I couldn't remember stuff, and it was just easier to go along with that opinion than to try to argue the point."

The doctor just looked at him expressionlessly for a moment. He then took out his light and started examining Norman's eyes. Taking a step back, the doctor said, "So, you never had memory loss?"

"No! However, you are the only one who knows that. Everyone else around here thinks the last 10 years is a big blank for me."

Doctor Karius leaned on the small counter as he asked, "But why maintain this farce?"

The shock of the concept finally forced the doctor to shut up for a second and actually listen to what Norman had to say. Norman tried to take advantage of the opportunity to explain his reasoning and initial findings in a manner that the doctor could understand.

Gazing at Norman with mild shock and a small touch of admiration, Doctor Karius slowly responded, "You need a new inner circle of friends and business associates!"

"You're telling me! This has been a tremendous learning opportunity for me. Sure, there were a couple of folks that I halfway expected to take advantage of the situation while others..."

Politely interrupting, the doctor asked, "How long is this memory loss of yours going to continue?"

Norman smiled as he answered, "Oh, I expect to make a full recovery within a week or two. It is very stressful remembering what I'm not supposed to remember."

Looking over the test results and the examination notes, Doctor Karius told Norman, "All of your readings are fine, and the swelling seems to have reduced, and the bruising is healing satisfactorily. I guess you're well enough for me to sign off on you. As for pretending to have problems with your memory—I caution you against it. Being honest with people is usually the best game plan."

Norman stood as he replied, "I totally agree—the truth is always the best route to take. However, there's a story I heard a while back. I don't know if it's true or not, but it sort of describes my current situation. A police chief in some small town was cleaning out his garage one day. He happened to come across some old toy that had belonged to his son years earlier. It was a strange-looking plastic box with a plastic antenna sticking out of it. The police chief discovered that there was a small button on the bottom of the box that caused it to vibrate slightly and make a loud buzz."

"Meanwhile, one of his police deputies stopped by to say hello. The deputy saw the strange-looking toy and asked what it was. The police chief was quite the prankster and quickly told his employee that it was a new drug-detector device that the FBI had just invented and had sent to him to test for them."

Norman tilted his head as he continued telling the doctor his story. "Naturally the deputy didn't believe the story at first. Until, that is, the police chief pointed the antenna towards the deputy and discreetly pressed the button on the bottom of the box. As soon as the box made its sound, the deputy turned white as snow. The police chief pretended to be seriously concerned as he pointed the toy towards the deputy again and pressed the button."

"The chief somberly asked the deputy if he had drugs on him. It was all the chief could do to keep from laughing until the deputy asked how the little box knew. As it turned out, the deputy really did have a small bag of cocaine on him. And the police chief's prank discovered the truth weeks and possibly months before they would have found out about the deputy otherwise."

He took a deep breath before telling the doctor, "I guess what I'm saying is that I don't look at my alleged memory loss as being a lie but rather as a prank that is revealing a lot of wrongdoing around me. I'll regain my memory as soon as I find all of the metaphoric drugs the folks around me are trying to hide. So, if you could keep my secret for just a couple more weeks, I'd really appreciate it."

"I won't lie for you. However, I guess there is always doctor-patient confidentiality."

As the two men headed towards the reception area, the doctor thanked Norman for leveling with him.

Norman laughed as he replied, "I was worried that you'd schedule me for a frontal lobotomy or electric shock or some worse treatment if I didn't come clean with you."

Walking into the lobby, Norman was shocked to be suddenly greeted by Freddie. "Hey, Norm! How's everything? So, Doc, is he doing well?"

Doctor Karius smiled at Norman as he answered Freddie. "He seems to be doing well. Norman, if you experience any issues, please let me know. Have a good day."

Before the doctor could slip away, Freddie urgently asked, "Doc, how much longer before my brother gets his memory back?"

The doctor and Norman exchanged glances, and then the doctor delivered a calculated response. "I wouldn't be surprised if a couple of weeks from now he remembers everything in full detail. Now, please excuse me; I really must get on with my rounds."

Norman looked at his brother and asked, "Freddie, what are you doing here?"

Distracted, Freddie hesitated until he eventually said, "What? Oh, I wanted to talk to you. I heard you were going to be here, and I thought we'd have time to talk before the doctor saw you. Who knew you'd get in so quickly, right? I mean, after all, it is a doctor's office. I figured we'd have plenty of time to talk."

Norman just shook his head and headed for the door. "I don't have time to talk to you now. I want to go to the office and get caught up on some things."

Freddie excitedly replied, "Great, I'll meet you there."

Before Norman could warn Freddie not to expect to talk to him at work either, he had already darted away to the parking lot. Norman was again left just shaking his head in frustration. Why wouldn't Freddie just leave him alone?

Once at his office, a flurry of activity surrounded Norman as he tried to get settled in his office. Freddie was snaking his way into Norman's office as one clerk was delivering a handful of phone messages, and Nadia handed over several files.

Norman was not firing on all cylinders yet and was probably only hearing half of what everyone was telling him. He did happen to make eye contact with Nadia as she handed over the files. She said, "Glad you came back when you did."

He smiled appreciatively, thinking it was a simple welcome-back remark, but then started wondering if perhaps there was more to the message.

Freddie started talking, but Norman was trying hard to tune him out as he read his messages.

Stepping towards the desk, Freddie asked, "So, what do you think of our new acquisition?"

Norman pressed the intercom and asked one of the clerks, "Hatty, did Meredith ever send over the final numbers for Lark Hardware?"

She said that she would check. Norman then started reviewing the files on his desk.

Freddie again started talking. "I think it's a great opportunity, and I'm sure you'll be pleased once I get going with it."

Norman retrieved a pen from his desk drawer and started making notes in the files.

Freddie took another step closer to his desk. "I think this is a great way to prove myself to you and make us all some money in the process."

Only catching part of what he had said, Norman looked up and asked, "Can't you see that I'm busy? I really don't have time to spar with you over your wild schemes."

Freddie started to respond when Patrick came into the office. "Did you tell him yet?"

Norman was becoming very annoyed by the distractions. He stood and was about to demand that they both leave when it finally occurred to him what Patrick had just asked Freddie. "Did he tell me yet, what?"

As Freddie shook his head, Patrick blurted, "It's a done deal! The papers are all signed, and we got it! If I'm not mistaken, that's the file on your desk."

Norman looked at the stack of files Nadia had brought in and saw the company name: "Too Perky Coffee." Picking up the file, he fell back into his chair and started reading it. All the while, both Freddie and Patrick bragged about how great of a deal it was and how much Freddie really did to secure the agreement.

Reviewing the paperwork, Norman slowly said, "This says that we collectively purchased this business—I didn't sign any agreement."

Freddie nervously looked at Patrick, who quickly interjected, "Norm! That must have been part of your memory that you forgot." Patrick walked over and lifted some pages in the file to show Norman the sales agreement. "See? There's your signature right there. You were hesitant at first, but once you saw the potential, you jumped at the chance to sign."

"That's right, Norm." Freddie nervously added as he cleared his throat. "You asked Patrick for sales numbers for the past 12 months. Once you saw how well they were doing, you were eager to sign."

Norman could feel his blood pressure rising and his face turning red with anger. He fought to calmly process the information before lashing out. As he came to terms with the realization that one of these guys forged his signature while the other helped to conceal the fact, he asked, "Is this the business we are in?

Buying successful businesses? I thought we targeted ailing companies and worked to help them get back on their feet."

Patrick smiled broadly as he patted Norman on the back. "There's a first time for everything. Isn't that right?"

Freddie smiled as he said, "It was a really fast-moving deal that you didn't want to slip away."

With his composure starting to fray, Norman angrily asked, "Freddie, when exactly did you become a voice in which acquisitions my company makes?"

Freddie saw an opportunity to claim Norman had already made him a partner and started to say so when Patrick interrupted him. "Norm, don't you remember? You brought him in just for this deal. You didn't say so exactly, but I thought if the deal went through that you promised Freddie a partnership."

Freddie quickly agreed. "That's right. Now that the deal has gone through, we can talk about that partnership."

Norman was fuming at this point and wanted to punch both of them. He realized he needed more time to plan an appropriate response. "Can you please leave now? I have a terrible migraine."

With a look of concern, Patrick asked, "Really? Maybe you came back to work too soon. You think you should take a few more days off?"

Norman quietly pointed towards the door, instructing Patrick and Freddie to leave. As they closed the door behind them, Norman fell back into his chair as he tried to grasp the magnitude of their deception. He knew that if he had come clean with his own little charade of pretending to have lost his memory, they would have just brushed it off as some type of post-traumatic episode and insisted that he really had lost his memory. If Norman had ever had a prank go more terribly wrong than this one, he certainly could not recall what it might have been.

His mind needed to wander to a happier place. Before he knew it, he was thinking about Leila and their lengthy discussions. He thought about all of the encouragement he received from her as well as from Walter and Emit about breaking away and moving to Ellensburg. Right now, moving away from all of these scoundrels was sounding really good.

However, as he had told his friends at the reunion, he didn't want to just run away. He wanted to teach them a lesson before he made a clean start elsewhere.

Being the methodical planner that had made him such a successful businessman, Norman knew he needed to do some research before making any rash decisions. Once his blood pressure returned to normal, he called his accountant, Meredith McKnight.

"Norman, it is really good to hear from you! Are you okay after your accident? We were all very worried about you."

"Thank you—I'm fine, really. The reason I'm calling is because…"

Meredith interrupted. "It's about Too Perky Coffee, isn't it? I told Patrick that there are more than a few red flags with that business. I told him I was going to tell you all about it, but that's when he told me about your accident. Are you sure you're well enough to be back at work so soon?"

"Seriously, I'm fine. The reason I was calling…Wait a minute. What red flags did you find with the coffee chain?"

"Just looking at their profits over the past several months, they continue to have spikes when they aren't showing corresponding increases in supply costs. If they are selling more coffee, wouldn't their costs for coffee and cups also increase?"

Norman suggested that they might have had surplus supplies and were just reducing on-hand inventories.

"I thought of that, but if they have a surplus in inventory, why are they continuing to order these supplies at a consistent pace? Also, I see where they are depositing large sums of cash into their accounts; $9,750 in May, $9,500 in June, $9,800 in July, and so on. There is no explanation where this money is coming from."

Norman quickly asked, "Nothing over $10,000?"

Emphatically, Meredith replied, "No! All these transactions are just below the mandatory reporting limit. Do you think they are laundering money through there, or something?"

Not having an answer, Norman decided to move forward as he said, "Hopefully, this won't be my concern. The reason I called was to ask you to review the books and give me a rough idea of the value of my stake in this company."

Meredith was a little confused. "Your share of the coffee shops?"

"No. My share of my company—my partnership with Patrick. What is the current value of it?"

"Norman, are you thinking of selling? Why?"

"Listen, Meredith, you were my accountant before you were the accountant for my company, so I know you'll keep this confidential. Let's just say that my accident helped me to reevaluate the priorities in my life. I'm just gathering information so I can make an informed decision. How soon can you get me a rough idea of my half of the company?"

Meredith corrected him. "You mean your 51 percent, don't you? I'll have something for you by tomorrow afternoon."

His next call was to his lawyer. Brian Nolasco was a good friend who had assisted Norman on several business legality issues over the years. For this reason, the sudden invitation to meet for dinner later that evening was not unusual.

For the rest of the afternoon, Norman tried to focus on the daily activities, but all the while he was making notes to himself about customers he would need to contact before he sold out, or precautions he wanted to take before severing his partnership with Patrick.

Hearing a light knock on the door, he looked up to see Nadia through the window. He motioned for her to come in. Inquisitively, she peeked over towards his computer screen to see if he'd logged on yet. Norman noticed her looking and asked if there was a problem.

"With your memory, well you know, I was just wondering if you needed help getting logged onto your computer."

Relieved that he hadn't already logged on, opening himself up for a bunch of questions about how he remembered his codes, he just laughed quietly as he said, "Yes, well, I was trying to figure out how I was going to sign on. Do you know my password?"

Nadia scoffed, "No. I don't know anyone's codes. I just know how to reset it so you can enter new codes."

As she went about the task of getting him access to his computer, she took the opportunity to bring Norman up to speed on a couple of issues that had been troubling her. "Your brother has sure been around a lot. He and Patrick seem to really hit it off well."

Norman just casually agreed as she rambled on.

"And your sister-in-law sure is nosy, isn't she?"

Norman raised a brow and asked, "Brandi? Why was she snooping around here?"

Nadia finished resetting his password as she answered, "She just asks a lot of questions about your business and Patrick's business, but mostly she was asking a lot of questions about Too Perky Coffee and why you didn't want to buy them."

Norman tried to understand Brandi's keen interest in his business and asked Nadia, "So, what did you tell her?"

"I told her that if she really wanted to know what your motivation was to do the things you do, then she should be asking you."

Norman smiled and said, "I bet she didn't like that too much."

"No, not at all. She finally left me alone when I started answering all of her questions with my name and position title.

Norman laughed. "So, you only gave her your name, rank, and serial number, ah?"

As she headed for the door, Nadia turned and replied, "Name and position only—I don't trust her enough to give her any of my numbers!"

It was early evening when Norman arrived at the small rural steakhouse for his meeting with Brian. The two friends caught up over a drink at the bar while they waited for their table. Both men individually suspected that the other had something important to discuss.

After they finally got situated at their table and placed their orders, Brian asked, "I'm kind of surprised you picked this place for dinner. I would have thought you wanted to meet quickly somewhere closer to home."

Norman glanced around the restaurant as he replied, "I like this place. It's quiet and away from the fast-paced city. I guess it's all part of my journey of rediscovery. You knew that I grew up in a small town, didn't you?"

"You could have fooled me. I thought you were a Denver transplant."

Norman chuckled as he shook his head. "No, Denver was just a temporary stop along the way."

Brian leaned forward with a determined look. "Listen, Norman. I'm glad you wanted to meet tonight because there is something I've been meaning to talk to you about. I think it would be best if you and Patrick found another lawyer for your business affairs. I'll continue to be available as your personal attorney, if you still wish. I just think there are some conflicts for me trying to serve your best interests and taking direction from Patrick regarding business matters."

Norman smiled slightly, which puzzled Brian. "I couldn't agree with you more. Let's take Patrick out of the equation." With a small chuckle, Norman continued, "This is why I wanted to meet with you tonight. I want you to draw up a contract selling my 51% of the business."

Brian interjected, "You are selling to Patrick?"

"Maybe, but I'm keeping my options open right now. So, for now, we'll leave the buyer's name blank. Since I'm asking you to do this, I want you to structure it for my best interests. There will be no non-compete clauses. In addition, I want to retain my individual clients in addition to any of our joint clients who want to follow me to my own company."

Eagerly, Brian suggested, "You want me to go ahead and file your paperwork for your new company? If so, I'll just need a name and address to get the ball rolling."

"Yes! I want you to handle all the legal details. Now, as for this purchase of Too Perky Coffee, I need to make sure I am totally separated from that acquisition and protected from any future ramifications that may arise from it."

Brian appeared to relax significantly after hearing this. "You are wise to distance yourself from it. There are too many things about it that just don't add up."

The two friends began to plot the best strategy for Norman to liquidate his holdings in the company. As the evening continued, Norman let Brian know everything that he'd been through over the past few weeks. This helped Brian understand the various motivations involved as well as the new directions Norman wanted to take with his life.

To a large degree, this was the first time Norman had actually verbalized his plans in any specific detail. Doing so served to comfort him with his decisions. By the time the after-dinner coffee was served, Norman was feeling very satisfied with the idea of moving back to Ellensburg.

After dinner, Norman said goodbye to his friend and headed for his car. Thinking about all of the evening's topics, he soon was on the phone to Leila. As soon as she answered, he began to barrage her with news about his plans to sell his business and move away from Seattle.

Unable to get a word in, she just giggled at his enthusiasm. Finally, when a brief opportunity presented itself, she spoke. "You sound happy?"

After a reflective moment, he agreed with her, "Yes, I am. Hey! That reminds me—I need a business address over there. Can you get me a post office box so my lawyer can process the paperwork to get my new company going?"

"Sure! I can do that tomorrow morning. What are you going to call your new company?"

Dismissively, Norman casually replied, "Oh, it'll probably just be my name followed by the words limited or incorporated or something like that. My lawyer will decide when he files the documents."

Leila thought about this for a second before saying, "You must really trust your lawyer! He could name your company any number of things that you might not agree with. Besides, don't you want the name of your company to tell your clients that you have a creative mind and can come up with innovative and fresh ideas to help their business?"

While her comments did give him something to think about, he had just pulled into his driveway. He chose to take her suggestion under advisement rather than discuss it further.

Chapter 8

Isidora

The next morning, Norman awoke with renewed energy. His mind raced with all of the various projects he had in the works: selling his interest in his business, getting his house ready to sell, finding a place to live in Ellensburg, and, of course, the actual move itself, not to mention the various schemes he was working on to teach some of the opportunists around him a lesson or two. He was almost giddy over his full plate of things to do.

Once he was ready to go to work, he went to the kitchen to get a cup of coffee and maybe some toast. There, he found Estella busy making her mother an impressive breakfast. Isidora sat straight in her chair as she quietly watched her daughter prepare her meal. She politely smiled and slightly nodded her head whenever Norman made direct eye contact with her.

"Buenos dias, Mr. Armstrong. You are just in time. I made my mother a nice breakfast, and there is plenty to share with you."

Norman started to graciously decline, but the delicious aromas were too strong a temptation. "Well, only if you are sure there is enough for all three of us."

Again, when Norman looked at Isidora, she smiled and nodded her head with a single bob before resuming her blank expression.

Norman and Estella made small talk through breakfast while her mother ate in silence. Once she had finished and began sipping her coffee, Norman felt her stare. Like before, whenever he looked at her, she just smiled.

Estella didn't seem to notice Norman's growing uneasiness with her mother's manner. He just reminded himself that she was only going to be there a short while, and that in a week she'd be gone. Two weeks at the most.

When they heard a knock at the door, Norman was going to answer it, but Estella jumped up first and darted towards the door. Awkwardly, he tried to engage Isidora in conversation. "This sure was a delicious breakfast."

Isidora didn't appear to understand anything he had said.

"She must've got all of her cooking talent from you."

He hoped she was beginning to understand him when she put her cup down and leaned forward to speak. In a heavy accent, she said, "Buenos días, Mr. Armstrong."

Estella walked through the kitchen carrying a canvas bag as she made her way towards Dillon's room.

Shortly afterwards, she passed through the room again as she headed back towards the front door. This time, she was carrying a saxophone.

Curiosity got the better of Norman, so he rose from his chair to investigate as Estella was returning to the kitchen. "What was that all about?" he asked.

As she returned to her seat, she explained, "That shy neighbor boy..."

Norman interjected, "You mean Blake?"

"Yes, Blake. Anyway, Dillon told him that if he gave Dillon his camping gear, then Dillon would return his saxophone to him."

Norman ran to the front door in hopes of catching Blake for a more detailed explanation. He was too late since Blake was already gone. Now thoroughly angry at Dillon, Norman marched into Dillon's bedroom and grabbed the canvas bag and began yelling at him. "Whatever made you think you had the right to steal from people? It is theft, and I will not tolerate you using my house as your base of criminal operations."

Dillon groggily mumbled, "Can you keep it down? I didn't get in until late."

Norman raised his voice louder as he shouted, "Stop bullying Blake! In fact, leave him alone!"

Dillon noticed Norman was walking out of the room with the canvas bag. "Hey, wait a minute. My friends and I are going camping, and I need that stuff."

Norman looked back at Dillon and firmly stated, "You got money from your mother to go to a concert. You then got money from me to go to the same concert. As a result of your little racketeering operation, you can easily afford to buy your own camping equipment without having to extort the neighbors' children for it!"

Norman slammed the bedroom door shut as he headed back towards the kitchen. Estella and her mom heard Dillon yelling from his room. "You're not my father! You can't tell me what to do!"

Estella nervously told Norman, "That Dillon is a handful."

Before drinking the last of the coffee in his cup, he replied, "Tell me about it. I really can't wait until he moves out."

Seeing Isidora quietly sipping her coffee, Norman turned towards Estella and asked, "Please apologize to your mom for all of this tension. She really deserves a more peaceful experience while she stays here. I'm very sorry and embarrassed by it all."

After thanking Estella for the wonderful breakfast, Norman took the canvas bag back to Blake.

When Blake answered the door, he was surprised to see Norman but was scared to see that he was holding the canvas bag filled with camping gear.

"Blake, I believe this is yours. I just want to return it to you."

Blake looked towards Norman's house as he said, "Mr. Armstrong, if it's going to keep Dillon from coming after me again, I would rather he just kept this stuff."

"Blake, listen to me very carefully. Dillon will not bother you anymore. If he does, I want you to let me know immediately, and I'll fix it. Do you understand me?"

"So, you want me to be a tattle-tale. How will that make anything better?"

"Blake, I'm really trying to help out here. I want Dillon's bullying to stop once and for all. I'm asking for your help to give me feedback on how it's going. OK?"

The boy looked down at the canvas bag and then glanced back towards Norman's house. "Well, I guess if you asked me questions and I answered them, then it wouldn't really be telling, right?"

Norman patted Blake on the shoulder as he said, "Sounds like a deal to me. Now, I gotta run—I'm late for work. Thanks."

Once at work, Norman appeared to be going through his normal daily routine; however, he was busy making arrangements to liquidate his holdings and make a fresh start in Ellensburg. While some clients could easily make the transition, others were under contract and would require some legal manipulations. These files were set aside for Brian's review and recommendations.

Throughout the process, Norman was adding notes to his list of things he needed to do before he started the process of breaking away. At least twice, Norman had to refrain from bursting out in laughter since he was enjoying his progress towards his independence from the partnership.

All of his enjoyment came to a screeching halt when his brother strolled into his office demanding to know where his desk was.

With a puzzled look, Norman asked, "Your desk? What do you mean—your desk? Wouldn't you have to work here to need a desk?"

"Man! Don't you and your partner communicate? Patrick made me a business partner. So, where's my desk?"

Leading Frederick out of his office and into the clerk's area, Norman smiled confidently as he pointed towards Patrick's office. "If Patrick made you a partner, then you will need to see him about a desk. While I'm thinking about it, be aware that any compensation you believe you are due will be coming out of Patrick's half of the business and not mine. Are we clear?"

Before Frederick could respond, Nadia snorted as she tried to suppress her laughter at the way Norman handled the situation. Frederick gave her an evil glare right as the phone rang.

As she greeted the caller by name, Norman began retreating towards his office as he waved his arms signaling her to tell the caller that he was unavailable. As she began to take a message, Norman returned to his office, and Frederick demanded to know who was on the phone. Nadia tried to ignore Frederick, but he insisted on taking the call. Since it was a salesman, Nigel Tilghm, and not a client, she didn't see the harm.

Plopping down at a vacant clerk's desk, he took the call. "Hello, this is Freddie Armstrong. How may I help you?"

Nadia chuckled as she thought about how disappointed Frederick must be that he got a salesman rather than a client in need of some type of business solution. Her amusement faded to curiosity as she watched him become engaged in a lengthy conversation with Nigel. Maybe he did know what he was doing after all. She thought only time would tell.

The call Norman was waiting for finally came when Meredith phoned to tell him the estimated value of his portion of the partnership. They discussed several factors that he would have to keep in mind as he navigated the tricky waters of selling his interest.

Before ending the call, Meredith added, "You do know that once you sell, I will cease all dealings with your partner, don't you?"

Norman paused a second before asking, "You'll still be my accountant, won't you?"

With a mischievous tone, she replied, "Why, of course I will! However, I may have to increase my rates."

"Let's just focus on keeping my new business ledger off of life support, and then we'll discuss your fees."

After hanging up, Norman made a couple of notes before heading over to Patrick's office. As he approached, he could see May Landy through the window forcefully telling Patrick about something. All the while, Patrick just kept smiling at her as he tried to calm her down. Undaunted by all of the apparent drama, Norman knocked on the door before walking inside.

His sudden presence seemed to annoy both May and Patrick to varying degrees. Perturbed, May pointed her finger at Patrick and exclaimed, "This isn't over!" She then turned and stormed out.

Norman asked, "Her husband owns that fishing boat company, doesn't he? Is everything all right?"

Patrick glanced out the window as he watched May leave the building. "What is it, Norm? I've got things to do."

"This will only take a minute. I just wanted to let you know that I am selling my 51 percent of our partnership. In order to do..."

Patrick stammered. "What? You're selling out? You can't be serious."

Norman nodded his assurance that his mind was made up.

"Is this some immature reaction to us buying Too Perky Coffee?"

Norman smiled at the audacity of his partner accusing him of being immature. "Patrick, it's just time for me to move on. It's clear that we have different objectives. Selling will be in the best interests of both of us."

Norman took a step towards the door before turning back towards Patrick, saying, "I will be accepting sealed bids if you are interested in making an offer. The deadline for the bids to be in my hands is one week from today at 12 noon. I must receive full payment within 48 hours of bid acceptance."

With an added bounce to his step, Norman returned to his office. It was now time for him to make his next notification. Rather than calling Frederick, he called his sister-in-law Brandi instead.

"Brandi, this is Norman. I'm calling to inform you that I am selling my entire ownership in my business. I will be accepting sealed bids one week from today at 12 noon."

When it finally sunk in, Brandi immediately started to protest. "Wait a minute! I only wanted a piece of your business—not buy you out."

Norman playfully responded, "What's the matter? I thought you said Frederick could do this job. If that's true, he can do it with or without me being here."

Frustrated and slightly confused by the suddenness of this information, she tried to gain clarification. "Hold on a minute! There's a big difference between working with you and being part owner."

Norman slightly chuckled as he said, "I called you because, as you already let slip, it was always about what you wanted and not necessarily what Freddie wanted. It was you who wanted a piece of my business."

Brandi tried to argue the point, but Norman calmly shut her down. "It is not open for discussion. My 51-percent stake in the business is up for sale, and the bids are due at noon, one week from today. Most importantly, I must receive full payment within 48 hours of bid acceptance."

Again, Brandi started to argue with Norman, but again, he defiantly said, "Make an offer or not, I don't really care. The fact remains that once the funds are securely in my account, I will no longer own any part of this business."

If Norman didn't realize Brandi was extremely annoyed at him, he knew once she hung up on him.

He quickly called a couple of investors he knew for them to spread the word that he was accepting bids for his part of the business. He intentionally avoided notifying a couple of fellow consultants since he was friends with them and didn't want them getting stuck working with Patrick.

Feeling he'd achieved enough for one day, he headed home. Not long after leaving work, he got a call from Walter reminding him that Arm would be coming to his house the following morning to discuss his surveying needs. Norman thanked Walter again for arranging for Arm to help out.

Walter dismissed the thanks by simply saying, "No problem; besides, he owes me."

Before Norman could comment further, Walter asked, "So, tell me how it's going over there with your business and everything."

Norman then updated Walter on the forgery to buy Too Perky Coffee and his brother's involvement in the conspiracy. He also mentioned the lies they were both telling him as they tried to sell the deception.

He was about to tell Walter that he had put the word out that he was selling his part of the business, but Walter interrupted. "Sorry, Norman, I gotta go. Hope Arm can help you out tomorrow. Goodbye."

When his phone rang again, he thought it might be Walter calling him back, but he was happy to hear Leila's voice. The two casually talked for an hour about the reunion, all of the events at work, and their loose plans for the future.

She then raised her voice slightly as she exclaimed, "Hey! Where do you get off sending me to get you a post office box? They treated me like a terrorist or something."

"What are you talking about?"

"It seems that you can't just waltz up to the post office and get a mailbox. You need an address. I tried to explain that if you had an address, then you wouldn't need the box since you could just get your mail at your address. But no! They have their rules about such things. I thought they were going to call Homeland Security on me."

With a slight chuckle, Norman apologized for putting her into that situation.

"I finally thought to just give them my address. That seemed to satisfy them, so they then told me how much they wanted to charge you for the box. Let me tell you, they're trying to make the post office profitable from renting you this one box! The price was outrageous! So, I guess you'll just have to use my home address as your mailing address for now."

Again, with a laugh, Norman apologized for her trouble and asked, "Are you sure it won't be a problem using your address?"

Leila scoffed, "It'll give you a reason to stop by from time to time if only to get your mail. I'm looking forward to seeing you more than I did in the past several years."

Norman snickered at her playful attack. He then mentioned that he would pass the address along to his lawyer so he could complete the paperwork for his new business.

"What's your lawyer's name?" she asked.

"His name is Brian Nolasco. Why do you ask?"

She quickly told him some story about once dating a lawyer from Seattle and being curious if it was the same one. While Norman was skeptical that this was her true motivation, he noticed Isidora having difficulty getting in the house. He promised to call Leila the following day and rushed over to help his houseguest.

All of his questions provoked lengthy explanations in Spanish, which didn't help his understanding of what was going on. From what he gathered, Estella dropped her off at the curb as she went back to get something she had forgotten at the store. In her haste, she must have given her mother the wrong key to the house.

Norman didn't get the impression that Isidora was upset at the inconvenience since she continued to laugh occasionally throughout her rant. He was even a little amused at the graphic hand gestures that she used during her version of events.

When Estella finally arrived back from the store, Norman looked at her with intense relief as he told her, "I am so glad you came back. I really need to learn Spanish. In any event, I'll be in my room if you need me."

As he left the room, Estella turned and gave her mother a disapproving glare. Isidora quietly smiled and twinkled.

The next morning, Norman heard a truck door slam shut, so he went to investigate. He saw a man in work clothes grabbing some tools out of the back of his vehicle and then reviewing a file with several papers in it.

Norman walked towards him and called out, "Good morning. Are you the Justin Bieber fan?"

The man looked startled, either by the abrupt greeting or by the Justin Bieber reference or maybe even both. "No! Wait, did you see the video?"

Now, Norman was slightly puzzled. "What video?"

"Never mind. Anyway, Walter asked me to come look things over for you. I'm Armadillo Bue. Everybody calls me Arm."

Norman started to explain the situation, but Arm stopped him before he got going. "Let me determine the facts first, then we can start talking about opinions, OK?"

With that, Arm took off on foot to the other side of the street and began poking around along the sidewalk. Once he found what he was looking for, he drove a bright orange stake in the ground and then started walking towards the backyard.

Along his way, Bernardo popped out of the hedge and started lecturing Arm on where the property line should be according to his surveyor. Norman moved only enough to keep watch on the process. As Arm disappeared into the trees and shrubs along the back of the lot, Bernardo disappeared along with him. Norman heard another door shut and turned to see that it was Brian with a couple files of his own.

"Brian, this is a surprise. What brings you over here this morning?"

"I have the papers your associate asked me to bring over here today."

"My associate?"

"Yes. He said his name was Walter and that I needed to be here when the surveyor finished his job."

Norman was getting ready to comment when they both heard Arm and Bernardo walking towards them. Bernardo was still pressuring Arm to see things his way; however, Arm went back to his first stake and attached a laser light, which he then aimed directly towards the marker he'd just placed in the back. Arm then proceeded to drive at least three additional stakes in the ground along the path of the laser light's beam.

Bernardo was livid at the placement of the orange stakes. "Why are you putting these stakes here? This isn't the property line. It is clearly over there closer to his house. Don't you know anything about surveying? I have a good surveyor, and he found the line to be over there!"

Arm stood up straight and boldly looked at the loudmouth neighbor. "Sir, let me tell you that I am a fully licensed and highly experienced surveyor here in the state of Washington. In order to get my license, I had to pass several tests and have documented field experience in excess of eight years. In addition to all of this, I also had to successfully complete the Certified Federal Surveyor program. Now, if your surveyor friend placed this property line anywhere other than where I have it, he is either blind, incompetent, or both."

Arm motioned for Norman and Brian to come closer. Once Brian was introduced to the other men, Arm asked, "Brian, do you have the notices you were asked to bring?"

Norman was almost as much in the dark about these notices as Bernardo. They both looked on with great curiosity as Brian pulled some papers from his case. Then, with a look of a hanging judge, Brian started telling Bernardo the way things would be. "I don't know what kind of scam you were trying to pull in the wake of Mr. Armstrong's accident, but as you can clearly see, as evidenced by this official property line, Mr. Armstrong is not in possession of any of your property. In fact, it is you who are actually at fault by occupying his property. Obviously, your fence and driveway are on Mr. Armstrong's property."

Brian handed Bernardo a document as he told him, "This notice instructs you officially that you have 30 days to vacate Mr. Armstrong's land. In addition, it notifies you that your garage and gazebo are in violation of county zoning ordinances. I will be filing the necessary letters of protest with the county regarding those two structures. It will be up to them if they will require you to move the structures, pay some type of fine, or both."

Norman couldn't recall a time when he had ever seen Bernardo's face grow so red with anger. He turned and stormed back to his house mumbling incoherently to himself the whole way.

Arm told the two men that he would place several heavy-gauge metal markers in the ground along the property line just in case Bernardo decided to remove the orange markers. Before leaving, Arm looked at Norman seriously and asked, "Are you sure you didn't see the video?"

Norman assured him that he had not seen any video and thanked him again for his help with the property line.

After Arm left, Norman invited Brian in for a cup of coffee. They had various legal matters to discuss regarding the approaching dissolution of his business and the formation of a new business in Ellensburg. However, Norman, had to ask, "How did Walter know to tell you that the property line was too far over onto my land?"

Brian smugly replied, "I'm a great lawyer so I was prepared for all possible outcomes. First, I imagined what would be necessary if your neighbor was right, and you had to move the fence and give some land back to him."

"What if that had been the case?"

Brian pulled a file out of his case marked only with a single bold letter: C. "This file had the agreement for you to sign stating that you would move the fence within 90 days."

"You said 90 days? You only gave him 30 days to move everything off of my land."

Brian smiled and said, "Isn't it great having a lawyer on your side?" He then pulled out another file labeled: B. "This file has the documents stating that the fence was in the correct location all along. Since this would have meant there never was an issue, then these documents would have made your neighbor responsible for all the costs associated with the wild-goose chase he created."

Shaking his head slowly in amazement, Norman said, "When you saw the line cut across his driveway, you just happened to be ready for that too."

Isidora walked into the kitchen and quietly made herself a cup of coffee. Norman sprang to his feet and introduced her to Brian. She smiled and politely said, "Buenos dias."

Brian instantly saw an opportunity to practice his limited Spanish vocabulary and attempted to converse with her. She initially smiled at hearing her native tongue, but her smile diminished slightly as he struggled to complete his sentences.

Isidora launched into a moderate response demonstrating that Brian was in over his head. She took her coffee and quietly sat at the table while Norman and his friend continued to stand at the counter.

Norman discreetly asked, "What did you say to her?"

Slightly embarrassed, Brian replied, "I thought I asked her how her stay here was going and if she was having any luck finding a place to live. But now that I think about it, I may have asked if she ever danced with a parrot on her knee."

Norman rolled his eyes. "Great! It's bad enough that I can't say anything to her to make her feel more comfortable during her stay here, but now you go and give her the impression that I'm surrounded by idiots."

They both glanced over at her as she looked out of the window while she gently blew on her hot coffee.

Brian turned back and said, "Norm, I envy you. You have such courage and conviction in your life."

Norman just looked confused at his friend's remark.

"Think about it. I have this restlessness inside of me, but I'm too fearful to leave my comfort zone to do anything about it. Meanwhile, you get a notion that your life will be better elsewhere and immediately you pick up and move."

Norman was surprised at the revelation that Brian was in some way dissatisfied with his life. Before he could say anything, Brian said, "Maybe I should go skydiving or run with the bulls in Spain. Maybe this is just silly mid-life crisis type stuff I'm feeling."

They both laughed at the concept of Brian skydiving since he was scared of heights. As their laughter subsided, Norman adopted a serious tone and said, "Frost in the shadows."

Brian just looked at his friend, waiting for his explanation.

"Something I was reminded of when I went back for my reunion. On really cold mornings frost is everywhere. As the sun comes up, it melts the frost away from all the places it shines. The only place the frost remains is in the shadows. Maybe your angst is nothing more than frost in the shadows waiting for you to shine a bright light on it and melt it away."

With a scoff, Brian asked, "Are you saying you're my sunshine?"

Norman laughed as he answered, "Hell, no! I'm saying you need to produce your own sunshine and get your act together."

Suddenly, the two men heard Isidora loudly slurping her coffee. The three of them exchanged polite smiles along with friendly nods. Noticing the time, Brian announced he had to leave for another appointment and said his goodbyes.

After Brian left, Norman made eye contact with Isidora. There was something about her look. It was as if there was a sign of understanding in her expression. He quickly brushed it off since he too had to leave.

Chapter 9

Justice

Contrary to his expectation, the deadline for bids for Norman's share of the business quickly arrived. Norman doubted that he was totally prepared for the transition as he drove to work for the last time. Assuming there would be no issues with the winning bidder's financing, come noon, Norman would be free to move away and not look back.

As he pulled into the parking lot, he ran through all the things he wanted to accomplish before he left the office today. Seeing Brandi's car parked in his space triggered a chuckle as opposed to annoyance. He realized he had bigger fish to fry than to get upset over a parking space.

As he approached his office, he could see the door was open and Brandi was inside. Entering his office was not the reflective moment he had imagined since his sister-in-law's presence was a distraction.

She was apparently measuring the windows for curtains with the help of some handyman she had brought with her. After brief eye contact with Norman, she turned to her helper and said, "Obviously, this desk and chairs will have to go to the scrap yard. The carpet will need to be replaced, but we can hold off on that for now."

Norman was still not rattled by her brash behavior. "That's presuming that you will have the winning bid, isn't it?"

Brandi dismissed her helper as she confidently told Norman, "I have no doubt that we've outbid Patrick. Besides, I don't think he really wants to be a sole owner."

Norman slowly nodded as he asked, "Really?" He then opened his briefcase and pulled out three envelopes that he displayed clearly to her. "Assuming Patrick will be entering a bid, I believe there will be at least four bids."

He paused only long enough to savor Brandi's look of concern. He then asked her, "Did you come just to measure my windows, or did you bring your sealed bid?"

Curtly, she snapped back, "You'll have it before the noon deadline!"

As she stormed out of the office, Norman realized that his plans for the day were already off to a wonderful start. After a couple of minutes, Nadia knocked on the door and asked if Norman had a couple of minutes for her.

"Of course, Nadia. Please come in. What's on your mind?"

She closed the door behind her and then walked over to his desk. She quickly handed him a piece of paper as she told him, "This is my letter of resignation. I've thought about it a lot and decided that I don't want to stay here after you've left."

"I see. What are you going to do now?"

She shrugged her shoulders and sighed slightly. "I'm not really sure. Maybe I'll take a long vacation. Maybe I'll try to be lazy until after the first of the year and then try to find another job. I just don't know for sure yet."

With a tilt of his head, Norman asked, "What do you think of Ellensburg?"

Grinning, she asked, "Will it take me over an hour to commute to and from housing that I can afford?"

"No, you wouldn't have nearly that long of a commute over there, not even when it snows!"

Nadia laughed as she said, "I'll think about it."

As he walked her out of his office, he met Brandi as she marched towards him to deliver the sealed bid.

Always the professional, Norman asked, "Is this the sealed bid from you and Freddie?"

"Of course! What else would it be?"

Calmly, he asked, "Did both you and Freddie sign it?"

Stunned, Brandi fired back, "Freddie signed it—he's the one who is going to be the co-owner!"

Norman handed the sealed envelope back to her and told her, "Both of you will need to sign it. I will not accept it without both of your signatures on the bid."

She looked as if she was about to erupt. Snatching the envelope from his hands, she ripped open the envelope and quickly scrawled her signature at the bottom of the page. Shoving the bid back towards Norman, she blurted, "I'm really getting fed up with all of your game playing! I'll be very happy when this is all over with!"

Norman politely smiled as he responded, "Have a nice day."

Several minutes after Brandi made a dramatic exit from the building, Patrick walked into Norman's office and again tried to talk him out of selling. For at least five minutes, Patrick laid out all the reasons why Norman shouldn't sell. Quietly, Norman listened to his partner's rantings, mainly because he couldn't get a word in. As soon as Patrick ran out of steam and paused long enough for a response, Norman coolly asked, "Will you be giving me your bid now?"

Exasperated that his speech had not deterred Norman, he sighed heavily and pulled his bid out of his coat pocket. Handing it to his partner, he said, "I still think you are making a big mistake."

Before Patrick could leave, Norman asked him to wait for a minute so he could call Frederick into the office. Once the three of them were all in the office, Frederick started to sit.

Norman quickly said, "Don't get comfortable—this won't take that long." He then handed them both a document as he told them, "Please read over this and sign where indicated on the bottom."

As soon as they finished reading the paper, they immediately started protesting. "What is this? Certainly, you can't be serious!"

Norman's tone grew serious. "What's wrong, gentlemen? The document simply states that you both knowingly forged my signature on the coffee shop deal, and that you both conspired to misrepresent my involvement to the seller as well as to me. I think it's very straight forward."

Again, they both launched their individual protests as they told more lies to cover up their dishonesty.

"That's enough!" Norman barked. "It is really this simple. Failing to sign these documents will render your bids null and void. If you want my stake in this company—you'll sign."

Patrick took a step forward and asked, "What if neither of us sign?"

Without emotion, Norman said, "If you don't sign, I will contest the purchase of Too Perky Coffee as being fraudulent and expose you both to the public as the unethical shysters that you are. I would imagine that the previous owners of the coffee shops would then file their own lawsuits against you."

As both men signed their documents, Frederick looked embarrassed while Patrick looked angry. As they handed the documents back to Norman, Patrick asked, "What are you going to do with these papers?"

Norman reviewed the forms to make sure they were properly signed and dated before answering. "These are my get-out-of-jail-free card in the event of future possible lawsuits. There is something very peculiar about this coffee-shop chain. When it blows up in your face, this will protect me from getting burned in the fallout."

Patrick smugly said, "Buying Too Perky Coffee was an excellent business decision and will make this company profitable regardless of who owns it!" He then turned and left the office.

Frederick remained in the office as he summoned the courage to voice his opinion. "I think he's right, you know. I believe it was a great acquisition with lots of growth potential."

Norman just stood beside his desk looking at him with a blank stare.

Frederick started to leave, but then stopped to ask, "You knew I was lying about your signature all along, didn't you?"

Norman candidly replied, "Freddie, I've always known when you lie. You are a habitual liar. Growing up, there were times when it seemed funny watching you weave your web of deceit. However, once you became an adult, well, now it's just pathetic. Maybe it's pathological, or maybe you just never learned how to face reality or accept responsibility for your actions."

Norman took a deep cleansing breath as he added, "But it doesn't matter what I think anymore, does it? At noon, when I open those sealed bids, you might be the new owner or maybe Patrick will make you some type of junior partner. The fact will remain that I will be gone, and you'll have to stand on your own two feet."

Nadia politely interrupted to tell Norman that he had a call waiting. Frederick started to say something, but Norman had already answered his call. Nadia escorted Frederick out of the office as she closed the door behind them.

The rest of the morning flew by. Before he'd realized it, the time to open the sealed bids had arrived. He set up a conference call with Brian and Meredith so he could read the bids to them as soon as he opened them.

The first bid he opened was from a former business associate who had previously expressed interest in buying into Norman's business. The amount he offered was too low to be taken as a serious offer.

The next bid he opened was from one of Brian's friends who was looking to start a consulting business. The bid amount was lower than the first.

Brian apologized for his friend, but Norman stopped him, saying, "This is a valuable learning experience for someone starting out in business."

The third bid was from Patrick. Contrary to Brandi's earlier opinion, Patrick was interested in being the sole owner since his bid was in the range of Norman's expectations. Meredith quickly pointed out, "That's still less than the estimated value of your share of the company, according to my calculations."

Norman agreed as he opened the fourth bid. With surprise, he stated, "It's from May Landy!"

"Who is that?" Brian asked.

"You know that boat company Patrick partnered with? Well, the owner of that boat company is May's husband."

With an inquisitive tone, Meredith remarked, "That's interesting."

Norman snickered as he added, "If you'd seen the heated discussions between Patrick and May that I've seen over the last couple of weeks, you'd think it was very interesting!"

After reading the bid, they learned that while she had made a serious offer, it was still less than Patrick's bid.

Now for the moment of truth. As he was opening the final bid, Meredith wished aloud, "I hope it's for at least the minimum value, for your sake."

Norman read over the bid and then announced, "Well, Freddie and Brandi got what they wanted."

The winning bid was in between Patrick's bid and Meredith's calculated value for Norman's share. Meredith quickly pointed out, "You don't have to accept any of these bids claiming that none of them met your minimum requirement."

Brian added, "On the other hand, not that you would want to take a greater loss, but you don't have to sell to the highest bidder if you feel it would be in the best interests of your clients that Patrick take over the business."

Laughing suddenly, Norman exclaimed, "Trying to choose the better manager between Patrick or Freddie is like trying to choose the least painful death between being burned at the stake or being eaten by a shark!"

They discussed a few more points before Norman instructed Brian to draw up the papers to sell out to Frederick and Brandi. Brian agreed to communicate all of the specifics to the bid winners, while Norman agreed to pass along the news to all of the other bidders.

Before ending the call, Meredith once again pleaded, "You don't have to accept these bids. You can advertise more extensively and get a wider pool of bidders who will quite possibly exceed the current value of your holdings."

"I appreciate your opinion and agree that waiting could produce more interest. However, I also know that I'm getting, well, for lack of a better term, a lot of bad vibes about the state of this company. I just can't shake the notion that I need to sell now and make a clean break of it. You can call it irrational or impetuous if you like, but so be it. I'm selling out now and dashing off for a fresh start."

His friends told him that they understood his position and then started the work to finalize the transaction.

Before leaving the office, Norman swung by Patrick's office to break the news to him that Frederick had outbid him. He added, "With that being said, make sure your funds are ready just in case they can't produce the funds required in two days. In that event, it'll all be yours."

Patrick nodded as he thanked Norman for telling him in person.

As he drove home, Norman thought he would've been a little sad after selling his business and closing that chapter of his life. What he found instead was that he had a silly grin on his face that he couldn't get rid of. He was actually relieved and excited about starting over elsewhere.

Making his way from his car to his house, he glanced over towards Bernardo's house and saw him talking to some contractor wearing a hardhat. Norman chuckled as he thought about how he had obtained some level of justice for himself against his neighbor, his brother, his ex-wife, and his business partner. Now, if he could only figure out how to get his deadbeat stepson out of his house, things would really be looking up.

As Norman dropped off his briefcase and headed to the kitchen for a quick snack, he heard voices and laughter coming from the back of the house. As he went to investigate, he realized that they were coming from Dillon's room. He started to turn around and go back to the kitchen when a burst of laughter roared out from the room. Curiosity got the better of him, so he walked over and glanced in.

He was surprised to see Estella, Isidora, and several of their friends and family lounging around Dillon's room having such a good time. As soon as Norman noticed that Dillon was nowhere to be seen, Estella noticed Norman peeking around the corner. "Buenas tardes, señor Armstrong!"

With a look of intense curiosity, Norman entered the room as he slowly looked at all the folks inside. "Hello. What's going on? It looks like you are all having a party without me."

Estella started to explain, but her mother stopped her, saying she wanted to tell him. In perfect English, Isidora told Norman, "We are just celebrating our successful conspiracy to drive your stepson from your house." She then pointed at a couple of their friends and added, "We wanted to have the room totally cleaned out and taped for re-painting by the time you got back home, but we underestimated the damage Dillon had done. But, don't worry. Mateo and Tomas will have the walls ready for painting by tomorrow."

"You speak English!"

The sheepish smile grew as she replied, "I worked as an interpreter for a Chilean diplomat until he recently retired. I'm sorry for the deception; it just seems that I learn more about the people I meet this way. Please don't be too angry with me."

"Angry with you? I'm thrilled that you got Dillon to move out! How on earth did you persuade him to do that?"

They all started laughing again as they took turns telling Norman about their organized efforts. As soon as Norman left the house, they all showed up and gathered wherever Dillon was located. They would then talk very loudly in Spanish and tell jokes and laugh obnoxiously whenever they could. It cut his sleep short and interfered with his phone calls.

Estella chimed in. "I think yesterday's eight hours of salsa music did him in."

Mateo deviously said, "I'm sure the smell of Isidora's garlic fish helped to hurry his decision to leave."

Isidora laughed as she replied, "I hope so—I hate the stuff!"

Looking at Estella, Norman asked, "Why would you all do this? Seriously, it sounds like it took a lot of time and coordination."

"You're a good man, Mr. Armstrong. You know that I try to keep my opinions to myself, but when my mother and I heard him disrespecting you all of the time, well, we knew we had to do something."

Isidora said, "When he yelled at you that he wasn't your son, all I could think was how right he was. No son of yours would have turned out like he did. I'm sure of it."

Estella agreed, "She's right, Mr. Armstrong—he's not your son!"

In an effort to break the serious tone in the room, Tomas began to play some salsa music on his guitar.

"Stop, stop, stop, we had enough of that yesterday!" Estella exclaimed.

Isidora then asked, "Do you know any Bob Seger?"

Thursday morning had Norman prancing around like a much younger man. This was the day he was supposed to close the deal with Frederick and Brandi for his share of the business. Just when he didn't think the day could get any better, he got a surprise phone call from Leila.

He was anxious to tell her all about the latest developments with his family and job, but she cut him off. "Hey, Norm, I'd love to talk, but I'm kind of super busy right now. I just wanted to tell you that we have a date set for tonight at seven. I'll pick you up, OK?"

"Uh, yeah, sure. You're picking me up? What's the matter? Afraid I won't show up if you don't come fetch me yourself?"

Leila laughed briefly and said, "Yes, something like that. Listen, I really have to run. See you tonight!"

Norman was thinking about all of the possible restaurants she might be taking him to. Eventually, he started thinking more about getting to his office so he could close out his deal. All the way to the office, he imagined various possible scenarios of what he might encounter once he arrived. For each one, he set what he believed to be the best response.

Once at his office, his brother quickly approached and began to plead for more time to gather the necessary funds.

Norman picked up his phone and called Patrick. "Patrick, how soon can you have your certified funds if I accept your offer?"

Frederick immediately started waving his hands as he called out, "Wait! Wait! I was just asking a question. I have the money right here."

Norman ended his call to Patrick as he took the certified document from Frederick for closer inspection. Once he was convinced the document was legitimate, he asked his brother for the sales agreement Brian had sent to him.

Both Freddie and Brandi had already signed the sales agreement. Once Norman signed both copies, Patrick officially owned 49 percent, and Freddie and Brandi each owned 25.5 percent. Norman structured their ownership this way to keep Brandi from later claiming that Frederick had bought the company behind her back.

After gathering the last of his belongings, Norman said goodbye to the clerks and wished them well.

On his drive home, Walter called to ask if the sale was finalized. Upon hearing that it had been completed, Walter said, "Good! Glad to hear it for your sake. Listen, I've been doing some, uh, let's just call it system security testing. Anyway, I found some really strange emails between Mireya Henkel and Brandi Stone. Do you know either of these people?"

Norman quickly replied, "My brother married Brandi Stone—her name is Armstrong now. Mireya Henkel sounds familiar. She may be the lady who sold Too Perky Coffee to my former partner. Why would Brandi and this Mireya gal be emailing each other?"

Walter said, "From what I can see, they've been writing back and forth for the last few weeks. They obviously know each other. I get the impression they worked together at some point with some guy named Jian. It's kind of hard to follow at times, but it sounds like something happened to this Jian guy, and Mireya holds Brandi responsible. This was the leverage she used to pressure Brandi into facilitating a quick sale of her business."

Intrigued, Norman asked for more details. However, Walter said, "I was lucky to get this bit out of it all. Most of the notes were in some strange code or slang. All I know was that Mireya clearly threatened Brandi's current lifestyle if she didn't make sure the sale of the coffee shops went through. Brandi sent one note the night of your car accident telling Mireya that the sale was 'in the bag' since you were out of the picture."

Norman told Walter, "That is all very bizarre, isn't it? Why was Mireya in such a hurry to sell? What leverage did she have over Brandi? Did Patrick start his efforts to buy the coffee shops before Brandi's influence?"

Walter scoffed. "I can't answer any of those questions. What I do know is that only a defective product requires such coercion to get folks to buy it. I'd say you are one lucky guy to get out of all that mess!"

Laughing, Norman agreed.

Chapter 10

Wet Dog

Once Norman got home, he found a note from Estella telling him that she'd gone with her mother to the store for more paint. Evidently, repainting Dillon's room was requiring a heavy second coat.

Norman called Estella to ask if she could pick up a couple of things for him while she was at the store.

"We already left the store, Mr. Armstrong. We are at Five Guys now getting something to eat. We can go back afterwards, if you want," Estella explained.

"No, there's no need to go back. I was just trying to catch you before you left. Hamburgers sound good—can you bring me one?"

Defiantly, Estella blurted a simple, "No." Before Norman could respond, she added, "Your friend called the house to ask that I remind you of your date tonight. Leila said it was very important for you to be ready on time. Did you forget?"

Admitting that he had forgotten, he quickly thanked her for the reminder as he flew to get ready. As soon as he returned to the kitchen, he noticed a floral arrangement on the counter. It was probably something Estella had given to her mother.

Suddenly, the front doorbell rang. He quickly decided that Isidora wouldn't miss one of the long-stemmed flowers, so he snatched it out of the arrangement as he went to answer the door.

Norman jerked open the door and shoved the flower forward in hopes of impressing Leila. He instantly saw that it wasn't Leila at the door. It was a limousine driver who professionally announced, "That is a very nice-looking flower, sir. May I assume you are Mr. Armstrong?"

Composing himself, he confirmed the driver's assumption.

"Miss Leila sent me to collect you. Are you ready to go now?"

Norman stammered, "I wasn't expecting a limo. Suddenly, I feel so casually dressed for a chauffeured ride. Where is Leila? Where are you taking me?"

With a polite smile, the driver replied, "I am Lonna, and I will be your driver this evening. This is all Miss Leila has authorized me to say at this time."

Snickering, Norman slowly shook his head and said, "Well, we'd better go—we wouldn't want to be late for whatever she's planned."

Lonna opened the door for him. As he got situated, she pointed to a blank CD and said, "Miss Leila suggested you might be interested in the musical selection she prepared for you."

As Lonna closed the door, Norman took the CD and slid it into the sound system. Immediately, he recognized the music as being one of the songs his band used to play several years earlier. Hearing the song made him happy. He couldn't believe she still had a recording of their songs after all these years. When Leila sang her big solo, it took his breath away. She had always had such a beautiful voice, and he loved listening to it.

When the next song started, he started laughing to himself. The song contained one of his big bass guitar solos. When the dramatic part of the song began, he found himself playing some air-guitar there in the limo's back seat.

Listening joyfully to the song mix Leila had provided, he was puzzled by the third song. He didn't recognize it, but he did like it—a lot. The following couple of songs were also unfamiliar. All the new songs were enough alike that Norman assumed the same band performed them.

Sensing the limo had pulled off the interstate, Norman peered out to see if he could get his bearings. He knew exactly where he was as soon as he saw the big round wooden roof of the Tacoma Dome. He was very curious why Leila wanted to meet in Tacoma.

Once the driver navigated her way towards the back entrance of the Dome, he realized that he was going to some type of concert or show. Quickly looking out the other window, he saw the marquee in the distance. This was the night of the Kilo Hammers concert that Dillon and Blake had talked about so much.

Stopping at the back entrance, Lonna opened the limo door and announced, "Here we are."

Norman climbed out of the limo and thanked Lonna for the smooth ride.

As one of the security people approached them, Lonna handed an envelope to Norman. "Your stage pass and related documents are inside. I'm sure this gentleman will see that you get to where you need to be."

Rapidly absorbing all of the information, Norman turned his attention to the security man who greeted him. "You are Mr. Armstrong, I gather? Leila asked that I escort you to her as soon as you arrived. Please follow me."

As they serpentined through the maze of back-stage hallways, he nervously hung his pass around his neck. Suddenly, he heard his name being shouted by a familiar voice. He looked up just in time to see her run up to him and plant a big kiss on his cheek.

While he was replaying the kiss in his mind, she was talking a mile a minute explaining. "I told you that I sometimes get called in to help out when traveling backup singers get sick, didn't I? Well, that's what happened. Kilo Hammers has four gals who are backup singers. Well, one got sick." Leila lowered her voice as she looked around to see if anyone was listening. "Rumor is that she's in rehab. Anyway, they tried just using the three, but found that it just works better with all four. That's when they called me."

Norman started getting caught up in Leila's excitement and asked, "The songs in the limo—was that Kilo Hammers?"

After she confirmed it, Norman said, "These guys are great! They sound like a blend of Lynyrd Skynyrd and Government Mule, with a touch of the Black Crowes for good measure."

Leila excitedly agreed before asking how he liked the brief walk down memory lane.

"Where did you find those recordings? There've been hundreds of times that I've wanted to listen to them."

She laughed as she remarked, "I think our band had a lot of similarities to these guys. Just think, if we'd stayed with it, we might have been as famous as these guys are today!"

She continued to ramble on for several minutes. Norman realized that she was trying to burn off some of her nervous energy just like she used to back in their performance days, so he just let her babble without interruption. As she was about to harness her enthusiasm, the lead singer and drummer for Kilo Hammers walked by and asked how she was doing.

In a most professional manner, she assured them that she was ready to do her part to make the concert excellent. She then quickly introduced Norman to the two of them.

After a round of courteous greetings, Norman quickly asked the drummer, "I see you have a full array of Ludwig drums. Aren't most drummers these days using Pearl or Tama?"

The drummer paused for a second before responding. "Sounds like you know some stuff about bands. Yes, I prefer Ludwig. I always thought that since it was good enough for the likes of Ringo Starr, what could be better?"

"Led Zeppelin's John Bonham also seemed to prefer Ludwig."

When the lead singer asked how he knew so much about drums, Leila quickly answered that they used to have their own band. The drummer asked if he was a drummer too, but as Norman began to dismiss his abilities as a bucket-banger, Leila asserted, "He played the bass guitar like none other!"

The lead singer looked impressed as he asked, "What was your band's name?"

"Vicar Five was what we called ourselves. We just played a lot of local gigs, reunions, parties, dances at the local Moose Lodge, and the like."

The drummer looked at his lead singer and asked, "You hear that? Vicar Five—now, that's a band name! Who do we get as a warm-up act? We get Fwaumbwagos Bigun's! Half the flyers out there promoting our concert misspelled their name. When our manager first told us..."

Interrupting him, the lead singer looked at Norman and said, "Speaking of our warm-up group, they are getting ready to start the concert. Leila, you should find the other back-up singers and review the playlist. Norman, it's been a real pleasure to meet you. Make yourself comfortable back here, and we'll see you after the show, OK?"

Norman happily agreed and told them that he didn't want to interfere.

Before Leila left, she said, "This concert was sold out before they called me, or I would've got you a seat out front. This backstage pass was the best I could do for you. I hope you don't mind."

"Mind? I love it! Not that we ever played any venue this large, but it brings back a lot of good memories."

After she left, Norman took a peek at the audience. The place was packed, and the atmosphere was electric. He had no hope of seeing anyone he knew in the crowd, even though he knew Dillon was supposed to be there as well as Blake.

Several songs into the opening act had been completed when Norman was approached by a guy who looked like one of the stage crew. The guy pointed towards the stage as he asked, "How are they doing so far?"

Not knowing if this guy was associated with the Fwaumbwagos or not, he tried to be diplomatic. "For a warm-up act, I would've expected more of a beat and vibe to get the fans on their feet and fired up for fun. So far, it seems the fans are spending more time talking to one another and looking at their phones."

"Exactly! They're crap! We had an awesome group when we were playing down in Texas, but they had contract issues in Houston, so they couldn't finish the tour with us. You're Norman, right?"

Surprised, Norman nodded as he asked, "I take it you're with Kilo Hammers?"

With a friendly laugh, he introduced himself, "No one ever recognizes the bassist. Just call me Eeyore. I hear you played bass in your own band."

Within seconds, Norman and Eeyore were heavy into conversation about music, favorite brands of equipment, and the various riffs they each loved to perform. Eeyore led his new friend over to one of their sound engineers. "Norman, this is Cornbread."

"Cornbread?"

"The guys thought it was funny that I hold the record for the number of cornbread muffins eaten in one hour at the Cracker Barrel in Asheville, North Carolina."

"Very pleased to make your acquaintance, Cornbread."

"Cornbread tunes all of our stringed instruments before the show and then after each use." Eeyore then picked up one of his bass guitars and handed it to Norman. As Norman was admiring the guitar, he eventually tossed the strap over his shoulder. Eeyore took the headphones and suggested, "Please, play me something."

After grinning briefly at the chance to showcase his talent, Norman got serious and started to play a portion of a song where he had a solo part. He tapped, plucked, and slapped the strings as necessary.

Eeyore watched Norman's fingers intently as he listened. Norman and Cornbread both noticed that Eeyore was mimicking some of Norman's hand movements in an effort to better understand his technique. Suddenly, Eeyore picked up a second bass and began playing as well. Cornbread scrambled to blend the feeds so both bassists could hear.

Eeyore stopped Norman and asked if a different change-up would work better and then played an example of what he was suggesting. Norman got wide-eyed as he was inspired for a different spin-off riff. As he started exploring this new concept, Eeyore smiled as he too began creating a slightly new direction for the tune. In short order, both men were jamming with each other as they were inspired and prodded into a friendly competition of dueling bass guitars.

Cornbread got their attention when he shut off the headphones. He calmly pointed towards the stage so they could see that the opening act was over. Eeyore had to get ready to go on stage, and Cornbread needed to tune both bass guitars before the show. Before leaving, Eeyore shook Norman's hand as he said, "Thanks for the impromptu jam session. I hope we can talk after the show."

Leila and the other singers were making their way to the other side of the stage as they passed Norman. He exclaimed to her, "This is the best date night ever!"

She smiled, winked, and blew him a kiss.

Cornbread was having an issue with a couple of wires on stage and asked Norman if he would mind helping him out for a minute. Norman was eager to assist and jumped into action. As the two of them were wrestling with some connections to one of the amplifiers, they overheard two of the fans in the second row talking loudly to one another.

"Hey, Dillon, isn't that your father up on stage?"

Norman recognized the voice as one of Dillon's friends. He glanced over and made eye contact with Dillon right as he responded to his friend. "No, that's not my father! How many times have I got to tell you? My dad's in California."

Dillon leered at Norman as if to underscore his disdain for him and his recent eviction.

Cornbread noticed the interaction and realized it seemed to bother Norman for some reason. To distract him from whatever the issue was, Cornbread called out, "I think that's it. What do you think?"

Norman focused back on the task at hand and agreed. They both went back to the backstage sound panel where Cornbread ran a couple of quick tests before declaring that they had successfully fixed the problem.

Once everything was ready, the house lights dimmed, and Kilo Hammers took the stage. To overcome the opening band's lackluster performance, they started with one of their foot-stomping numbers. The crowd showed their enthusiasm with loud cheers and screams.

Meanwhile, Norman was admiring how Leila looked under the bright lights. He thought she was absolutely stunning, and her voice harmonized with the others beautifully.

Norman found a spot where he could enjoy the show without being in the crew's way. It'd been a long time since he'd been at a concert, and he was loving every minute of it. Between gazing at Leila and watching the other performers work their magic, he made himself useful by helping Cornbread move some instruments around when needed.

Cornbread laughed as he noticed Norman performing with his air-guitar off to the side during one of the numbers. Norman thought he was being mocked when Cornbread handed him one of the backup bass guitars and encouraged him to strap it on. Norman got a little embarrassed as he initially refused to take the instrument. However, Cornbread refused to take it back and just pointed up on stage. When Norman looked to see what Cornbread was pointing at, Eeyore was motioning for Norman to come up on stage and join in.

Norman started to protest, but Cornbread leaned towards him and said, "You'll end up on stage one way or another. Trust me, you'll wish you just went up now rather than waiting for them to shame you into getting up there later."

Deciding he didn't want to be shamed into it later, he went up on stage and plugged his loaner bass guitar in where Cornbread had instructed him. Eeyore pointed to a spot where he wanted Norman to stand as he told him, "I'll focus on the rhythm, and you can just fill in wherever you want."

Norman did just that. He started jamming like he'd been doing this for years. Making brief eye contact with Leila fired him up even more as he and Eeyore added a new dimension to the song.

When the song segued into the band's drum solo, Eeyore briefly discussed a couple of ideas with Norman about their role to join in after a few minutes. Norman was onboard and indicated that he'd follow Eeyore's lead. Norman didn't realize it, but this meant that he'd be sharing the spotlight with both his fellow bassist and the drummer.

Undaunted, the three of them had an incredible jam session that was supercharging the audience. The lead guitarist stood next to Eeyore as he joined in, and then the lead singer stood next to Norman as he began singing. As the other band members and backup singers also joined in, the energy in the Dome reached a fever pitch.

When the song finally ended, Norman immediately turned to Eeyore and thanked him for the opportunity to perform with him. Eeyore replied, "Our pleasure, but we're not done yet."

Before Norman could ask for clarification, the lead singer walked over and quickly shared some thoughts about how Norman could help boost the energy levels of the next two songs. "Norman, you're the jolt we needed to fire this crowd up after that snoozefest of an opening act—don't slow down!"

Norman laughed at being shanghaied into performing but was loving every bit of it. He quickly asked Eeyore, "I'm not stepping on any toes here, am I?"

Eeyore smiled as he shook his head. "Not at all. We're all about the music and never keep track of spotlight time."

This put Norman at ease as he flashed a wink towards Leila, who looked as if she was also having the time of her life.

After three more energy-infused numbers, the lead singer asked Norman if there were any songs he wanted to play.

"Do you know "Wet Dog" by Fredburg Snakes?"

Eeyore quickly played the opening chords of the song as the lead singer asked, "It starts with, 'You'll hug a wet dog, but you won't hug me...?'"

Norman happily replied, "Yes, that's it!" He turned to Eeyore and suggested, "I'll keep the rhythm and you jam to your heart's content, OK?"

Eeyore flashed a sly smile as he nodded.

Hearing which song they were going to play, Gus, the lead guitarist, came over and asked, "Did Jackson put you up to this?"

Not understanding the question, Norman slowly shook his head and proceeded to coordinate the instrumental start of the song with the drummer and Eeyore since the intro was a heart-pounding bass riff that was as challenging to play as it was quickly recognized by the audience.

The crowd was dancing in the aisles and stomping their feet in sync with the music. Just as the lead singer began to belt out the first lyrics, another guitarist came out on stage, and the crowd exploded into cheers. It was Jackson Sims, the lead guitarist for Fredburg Snakes. He immediately began jamming with the lead guitarist from Kilo Hammers on stage left while Eeyore and Norman were jamming on stage right.

It all looked highly planned and choreographed as the backup singers moved to flank the lead singer. No one in the audience realized that it was totally spontaneous and unscripted. Norman looked at Eeyore as if to ask if Jackson was a planned surprise guest. He just shook his head and indicated he was just as surprised as anyone else.

After the festive and lively rendition, the lead guitarist grabbed a microphone and introduced his friend. "Show some appreciation for Jackson Sims of the Fredburg Snakes!"

The lead singer then introduced all of the regular band members before adding, "Joining us from the group Vicar Five, we have two skilled performers. First, the lovely and talented Leila Martin singing with our chorus, and our guest bassist is Norman Armstrong."

The crowd cheered, but Norman was too modest to believe it was anything more than just alcohol-induced revelry. There wasn't time to appreciate it anyway since the drummer and Eeyore started the grand finale.

Cornbread came up on stage to adjust one of the amplifiers. Eeyore said something to him quickly. Cornbread then walked over to Norman and said, "If you haven't guessed, this is our finale. It's a 15-minute song that often gets stretched to about 20 minutes if the conditions are right. Considering the two guitarists are friends and fierce competitors, we might set a record length tonight."

Norman thanked him for the update as he stepped closer to Eeyore to follow his lead. During the 25-minute finish, the two bassists took turns keeping the rhythm or freelancing various riffs to complement the song. Meanwhile, as expected, the two guitarists were dueling it out as all the singers filled in wherever they could.

By the time the concert ended, the fans were hoarse from all of their yelling, and the musicians all felt they had given it all they had. Leaving the stage, Leila threw herself at Norman and gave him a big kiss.

Eeyore invited them to their after-party, and they both eagerly agreed. As they made their way towards the party room, one of the crew called out, "Hey Norman, there's some kid out here demanding to see you. He says he's your son."

Norman headed back towards the stage wing as he considered what he would do or say if Dillon was now willing to call him his father so he could benefit from it somehow.

The drummer had overheard that Norman's son was calling for him, so, as he walked past, he said, "Hey, Norman, it's okay if you want to bring your son to the after-party. He's welcome, too."

Norman smiled and thanked him even though he didn't really want to risk whatever embarrassment Dillon could cause. Nearing one of the final curtains separating the audience from backstage, Norman could overhear Cornbread talking to someone in a very firm tone. "Listen, kid, I heard you clear as day tell your friend here that Norman was not your father. Now you are trying to convince us that he is?"

Norman then heard Dillon's friend say, "Come on, dude—let's get out of here. They know he's not your father, so they're never going to let you in."

Dillon started to protest, but his friend insisted that they'd never get backstage.

Norman walked around the curtain in time to see Dillon and his friend arguing about whether they should continue the effort to use Norman for access to meet the band. Cornbread, seeing Norman, asked, "This kid is now saying he's your son. Do we let him in or not?"

Dillon noticed Norman standing there and hollered over, "Hey, Dad, let us in!"

Before he could answer, he caught a glimpse of a familiar face farther back in the crowd. He called out, "Blake, is that you? Come on over here!"

He then told Cornbread, "Here's my boy!"

Cornbread, Norman, and security moved the barrier apart just enough to let Blake through. As Norman and Blake made their way backstage, they heard a couple foul-mouth remarks from Dillon as security escorted him out of the building.

Blake quickly said, "I'll have to work hard staying out of Dillon's way after this!"

Norman laughed. "Don't worry about it. He's moved out of the neighborhood, and I don't think you'll be seeing too much of him ever again."

Thrilled, Blake started bombarding Norman with questions. "How'd you get to be on stage with Kilo Hammers? Did you know Jackson Sims was going to be here? Your band—Vicar Five, I never heard of them—did you play around here?"

Norman again laughed as he asked Blake to slow down a bit. "Try to control your exuberance. We're going to the after-party, and you can ask your questions there."

As they approached the entrance, Norman introduced Leila to Blake. The three talked for a few minutes primarily to allow Blake to calm down a bit before entering the party.

Leila cautioned Blake that taking pictures of the party would be frowned upon. Overhearing the suggestion on his way into the party, Cornbread said, "That's some good advice."

Cornbread walked just inside the door and called for a couple of the musicians to join him at the door. Then, walking back to where Blake was getting his after-party etiquette lecture from Leila, Cornbread lined up Eeyore, Jackson, Norman, Leila, and Blake for a group picture. Blake was thrilled that he would have at least one picture proving he met the celebrities backstage.

Eeyore started talking to Blake about music after hearing that he played the saxophone. Meanwhile, Jackson asked Norman, "I hear you were responsible for choosing to play "Wet Dog." Did you know I was here?"

Norman explained, "No, I had no clue. It's just a great song with a strong bass opening. When I was asked what I wanted to play, it was just the first song I thought of."

"I'm flattered and shocked! The timing was incredible. I just had time to say hello to my friend Gus right before he had to go on stage. I thought the song choice was his idea."

Norman was amazed and replied, "But you had a great time, right?"

Leila and Norman melded with the other musicians and crewmembers effortlessly while Blake continued to look like a child visiting the circus for the first time.

Almost an hour into the party, Norman asked Leila if he should be concerned for Blake. After Leila asked why, he pointed towards Blake, who was now surrounded by two of the backup singers and one female crewmember.

"Oh, that. Don't worry about it."

"Don't worry about it? I'm the one who got him into this. His mother is going to kill me if..."

With a tug on Norman's arm, Leila smiled as she interrupted him. "I said—don't worry about it."

"How can you be so casual? He's only a teenager, and those women are in their twenties."

"I can be casual because I know that the girl on the left is Gus' daughter, and he's not about to let anything happen to his baby girl. Besides, they're just playing cards."

Norman relaxed briefly before looking shocked. "They're playing strip poker!"

"I was hoping that you wouldn't notice that he and the girl on the right aren't wearing the shirts they came in here with."

As Norman started to walk over to chaperone the card game, Leila stopped him and said, "Look at him. I know I just met him, but I'd be willing to bet that he's not going to get rid of that smile on his face for several days. So, why don't you worry less about Blake and more about putting that kind of smile on my face?"

Eeyore and Cornbread were deep in a philosophical discussion about the extent people shape their own destiny as opposed to how much fate shapes destiny. Reaching a stalemate between their two opinions, they brought Norman and Leila into their lively exchange. Norman considered the various positions carefully and began to lobby for the role of fate as he looked at Leila as if to imply that it was fate that brought them back together after all of these years. At one point, the three men looked at Leila and asked for her thoughts.

After pondering for a brief moment, she answered. "Several days ago, I was reminded that people are like the frost in the shadows."

Eeyore said, "Frost in the shadows?"

Norman was pleased she remembered his remarks from their recent sunrise observance. Cornbread just wondered whether he needed another beer before listening to any more of this dialogue.

"Yes, frost in the shadows. We are like the frost in the shadows. The frost doesn't change on its own. The grass doesn't generate any heat to melt the frost. Even the trees and rocks that create the shadows where the frost resides have no bearing on what happens to the frost. Only the effects of the rising sun change the appearance and physical nature of the frost. The sun acts like fate influencing what ultimately happens to the frost. At least this is my opinion."

While Norman was impressed with how Leila took his earlier discussion and improved on it, Eeyore reflectively repeated the phrase, "Frost in the shadows, ah?"

Cornbread interjected, "Sounds like a good title for a song."

Eeyore and Cornbread started collaborating on how a song about frost and fate would sound while Norman gave Leila a hug and a tender kiss. As she leaned in for a more passionate kiss, Blake interrupted. "Mr. Armstrong, can you give me a ride home?"

Norman and Leila chuckled lightly at his poor timing as they turned to answer him. However, what Norman saw caused him to blurt, "Blake, where is your t-shirt?"

With a timid laugh, Blake pointed over towards where he had been partying with the young ladies. "Oh, they wanted to sign my t-shirt. They're getting a little carried away with drawing pictures and stuff. I'm going to frame it for my wall. Gus and Jackson both signed it too. Isn't that so cool? Anyway, I'm sure my ride already left, and I was hoping you'd give me a ride home."

Norman replied, "When you are fully clothed and ready to go…"

Leila stopped Norman and politely told Blake, "We'll be glad to take you home when you're ready to leave."

Blake thanked them both and added, "I don't think I'll ever be ready to leave, but I don't want to overstay my welcome."

The three of them agreed that they would leave in 10 minutes. This allowed them all time to express their appreciation as well as their farewells to the band. Blake was hugged and kissed by all of his new lady friends, and Norman and Leila were asked for their contact information. Eeyore and Gus both promised that if they toured again in the Northwest that they would call to invite them back. Jackson was very intrigued by Norman's work and wanted to stay in touch for possible investment opportunities.

It would have been an understatement to say Norman, Leila, and Blake all had had one of the best evenings of their lives. They were all grinning from ear to ear as they climbed into the limousine for the ride home. Blake had never ridden in a limo before and was clearly excited about the experience.

When they arrived back at Norman's house, he started to point out the various kiss-prints on Blake's face, but Leila squeezed his arm tightly, signaling for him not to do so. As Blake ran back to his house, Leila explained. "Either he knows his face is covered in kiss-prints and is content to keep them as long as he can, or he doesn't know about them. If he doesn't realize they are there, then when he looks in the mirror, he will have a pleasant time remembering how they got there."

Norman shot back, "I'm more concerned with the reaction I'll be faced with if his mom sees them and decides to hold me responsible for his corruption."

"Well, if you are really worried about it, maybe I should spend the night so I can help run interference for you."

Flashing a smile of acceptance for her suggestion, Norman tipped Lonna and dismissed her for the evening.

As they walked towards the front door, Norman said, "If you plan to run interference for me, maybe I should warn you about my mail carrier."

Chapter 11

No More Shadows

Many people would sleep in on a Monday morning if they didn't have a job to go to; however, Norman was too busy making lists and planning everything he needed to do. His mind raced as he prioritized the tasks he wanted to accomplish within an aggressive timeframe.

The smell of fresh-brewed coffee told him that Isidora was awake and in the kitchen. He hoped she'd made enough for two as he cheerfully greeted her. She waved in response as she sipped her drink.

"No! Waving and nodding are no longer acceptable, now that I know you speak English exceptionally well."

Isidora laughed as she replied, "I feel as though you will never forgive me for my deception."

They both laughed and made a few more quips about her initial charade. She then asked, "Didn't you have something to do with a coffeeshop?"

As Norman rolled his eyes and started to explain his involvement, he noticed she was pointing to the television on the counter that was on but muted. The news was airing some story about coffeeshops and they could see the logo of Too Perky Coffee on the kiosk behind the reporter. Norman quickly turned up the volume.

"…Snohomish County Sheriff's Department worked closely with their counterparts in King County for the past three months to gather the evidence necessary for this morning's filings. The charges include multiple counts of prostitution and money laundering, in addition to possession and distribution of narcotics. We were also informed that the federal government has been investigating this company and will be filing their own separate charges shortly…"

Norman was shocked by the news. As he started to say something to Isidora about the story, the news showed a picture of his former office.

"…Mireya Henkel recently sold Too Perky Coffee to a local business brokerage firm owned by Patrick Harbison, Frederick Armstrong, and Brandi Stone-Armstrong. Our sources were all quick to point out that Norman Armstrong, a former co-owner of this firm, had been on medical leave during the acquisition and was in no way connected to or involved with the now-shuttered coffee chain. We will update this…"

Turning off the television, Norman quietly attempted to process the information. Isidora quickly said, "You have some very loyal friends!"

He looked at her inquisitively.

"Well, someone made it a point to make sure you were kept clear of the mess. That reporter mentioned that their sources—plural— wanted to ensure you maintained a clean image throughout all of this."

Nodding slowly, he replied, "It was either that, or I'd show the document they signed exposing their forgery and deceptive business practices."

Taking a slow sip of her coffee, she retorted, "Then, you have a very good lawyer."

Norman agreed as he realized that he should probably call Brian to make sure he was aware of what was going on.

After a brief discussion with Brian, reality began to set in as to how close he had come to being wrapped up in the mess he was watching unfold. Norman wondered how much of this problem was his doing, because of the whole memory-loss prank. Would Patrick and Freddie still have forged his name on the sales agreement if he hadn't pulled that stunt? Could he have prevented the purchase of the coffee shop chain?

The doorbell interrupted his thoughts. He was happy to see Nadia smiling at him as he answered the door. "What a pleasant surprise! What brings you here?"

Nadia handed Norman a box as she answered. "I wanted to bring you some of the files you left behind, as well as some mail, and about a thousand phone messages that came in after you left."

Norman eagerly invited her into the kitchen for a cup of coffee. After he introduced her to Isidora, they all sat down around the kitchen table. As Norman started going through the box, Nadia said, "You left those client files at the office, but they all called and were adamant that their business arrangements were with you and not Patrick. They asked me to tell you that they aren't going to work with Patrick. So, either you continue working with them, or they'll find a different firm."

Norman quickly asked, "Did you ask these clients to do that?"

"I didn't have time to chew gum after you left—much less call clients! Each of these clients called me as soon as they learned you were no longer with the partnership."

"But I'm moving to Ellensburg. Certainly, they want someone closer..."

"Norman, you have clients from Weed, California, to Havre, Montana, and from Black Forest, Colorado, to Tofino, British Columbia. I think you can manage to continue helping these folks even after you move to Ellensburg."

Isidora smiled as she boldly announced, "I like this lady!"

Eyeing the plate of assorted fruit-filled pastries, Nadia asked, "Are those from that Filipino bakery over on Beacon Hill? Do you mind if I take one?"

Norman scoffed at the request as being unnecessary since she was welcome to have as many as she wished. He quickly replied, "Sure! Whatever floats your boat!"

Isidora struggled with the slang phrase, but before she could ask for clarification, Nadia blurted, "Boats! How'd I forget to tell you? The port authority is fining Freddie for a boatload of railroad ties that has been sitting at the port for over a week now. They've given him until the end of the month to move the entire shipment out of the port, or they claim they'll deliver it all to the office at Freddie's expense."

Shaking his head, Norman muttered, "So, now he's got the port authority mad at him too."

Talking with her mouth full of pastry, Nadia hurried to add, "The port authority is the least of his worries! It seems they are the only ones not trying to put him in jail!"

Washing down her food with a quick gulp, Nadia began counting out Freddie's issues. "He and Patrick have county and state officials investigating their involvement in the prostitution ring and how much they knew, or should've known, when they bought it. Next, Patrick has the IRS going after him ever since they got some tip about him embezzling funds from that fishing boat fleet he'd acquired..."

Norman interjected, "He's been involved with that company since before he partnered with me."

Briefly nodding in agreement as she continued counting out Freddie's and Patrick's legal issues, Nadia added, "Then they have the state liquor board after them for non-payment of liquor taxes on the three taverns they own in West Seattle. Freddie and Brandi claim that was before they became partners with Patrick, but the state maintains they should've seen the error when they reviewed the books before the sale."

Isidora asked, "Prostitution, embezzlement, bootlegging, and forgery. Were you business partners with these folks, or were you a member of a crime family?"

Norman slowly replied, "I'm beginning to wonder about that myself."

Nadia reached for another pastry as Norman slid the plate closer to her while Isidora freshened her coffee.

Norman wondered out loud, "I just can't understand how all of these things happened all at once."

Struggling slightly to swallow her last bite, Nadia replied, "I'm not sure where the information about the coffeeshop prostitution ring came from, or what the railroad tie business is all about, but the embezzlement and liquor tax investigations were the direct result of sworn statements from May Landy."

Norman asked, "Was that the lady who we saw getting upset at Patrick and then storming out of the office a while back?"

"Yes, that was her. Her husband is the owner of that marina over on Vashon or Bainbridge, I always get them mixed up. Anyway, Patrick kept leading her on, and she finally got fed up with his failure to commit. She started blabbing all she knew to any law enforcement agency who'd listen to her."

"Why didn't you tell me about any of this?"

"I just found out about it the day of your accident."

Loud noises from outside caused Norman to look out the window in time to see a bulldozer tearing up his neighbor's driveway. Bernardo noticed Norman looking and promptly flipped him off. Norman calmly smiled and waved at his frustrated neighbor.

Norman turned towards the two ladies in time to see Nadia eyeing the remaining pastries. Before he could speak, the doorbell rang.

"Wow, this is turning out to be a very busy morning!" Norman exclaimed as he went to the door.

"Brian! I just spoke to you on the phone—you didn't mention you were coming by."

"Didn't I? It's been so crazy this morning, I'm surprised I remembered to put on pants before leaving the house."

Leading the way to the kitchen, Norman offered, "Would you like coffee? I'm not sure if there are any pastries left."

Nadia flashed a guilty grin as she giggled a half-hearted apology.

Brian quickly opened his briefcase and started discussing business. "Norman, I need you to sign these forms at the bottom and then these forms where indicated. I also need your initials on this side over here…"

Norman, looking as if he were a deer caught in headlights, muttered, "What papers? What is all of this?"

"These are the forms to register your new business in Ellensburg. A couple of your associates called me with the specifics."

As Norman reviewed the documents, he slowly fell into a kitchen chair. "Associates? What associates? This says I'm the sole proprietor of Norman's Frost, LLC. What the…?"

Brian quickly interjected, "Listen, the name doesn't matter. If you don't like it, then you can change it easily enough. The important thing is to get these papers filed as soon as possible so your clients will know where to contact you."

Isidora calmly added, "Sounds like you already have a bunch of clients lining up to do business with you."

Nadia said, "They've all threatened to take their business elsewhere if you don't sign these papers."

After a little more prodding, Norman murmured, "Norman's Frost?"

At this point, Brian handed Norman a pen and pointed to where he needed to sign. Norman slowly shook his head as he signed the documents.

Isidora commented, "Like I said before, you must have good friends."

After his guests had left, Norman called Leila. "Are you one of my associates?"

She quickly laughed as he continued. "My lawyer says that my associates gave him the details of my new business."

Leila fought her giggles as she answered, "Of course I'm one of your associates! I'm your marketing manager."

"I gather I have you to thank for the name—Norman's Frost?"

In a slightly more sober tone, she asked, "You don't like it? It's a spin on our earlier discussion about frost in the shadows and such." She continued, "The farmers around here see frost and snow as a winter blanket protecting the ground during the harsh winter while the fields re-energize for the next year's crops. Isn't this what you do with the businesses you buy? You obtain, re-tool, re-energize, and then sell them. Essentially, you are the protective blanket."

Norman smirked as he simply said, "Well, it'll take me some time to get used to it."

Leila quickly added, "By the way, your IT manager has already set up your website complete with customer testimonials from current and former clients."

"My IT manager? You mean Walter?"

"Of course. Nadia said she'd pass the website address along to your current clients."

"She already knew about this?"

Leila laughed and quickly changed the subject. "Will I see you this weekend?"

Around noon, Norman went out front and began to survey the work required to pack up the garage. As he began to plan how he was going to attack the years of clutter that had accumulated in such a limited area, Blake walked up and began talking about the ruckus next door. Norman just smiled and nodded slightly.

"Blake, how would you like to help me clean out my garage? I'll pay you for your time. As a bonus, if we find anything of Dillon's that you'd like, you can keep it."

Blake readily agreed and immediately started to help Norman pull things out into the driveway. After several minutes, they heard a car stop in front of the house. Norman looked up to see Freddie getting out of his car.

Norman told Blake, "Looks like we'll be taking a small break."

Blake nodded and walked away.

Norman waited until Freddie was halfway up the driveway before coolly asking, "What do you want?"

Freddie flashed a nervous smile as he tried to sound friendly. "Hey, Norm. How you doing?"

Norman didn't respond.

Freddie stated the obvious. "So, you're cleaning out your garage?" He then suggested, "Maybe we could go inside, get a beer, and talk a bit."

"No. Now, state your business."

Quickly looking around, Freddie then struggled to apologize. "Okay, things didn't work out the way I'd hoped. I mean, how was I supposed to know how complicated everything would be?" He paused briefly before adding, "That Patrick sure is a slick one, ain't he?"

Freddie then flashed his favorite trademark "I'm so pitiful" expression. Norman had seen this expression many times over the years. While it frequently worked to soften their parents' anger over Freddie's wrongdoing, it had the opposite effect on Norman. It had always sickened him. It was his brother's get-out-of-jail-free card—his license to get instant forgiveness. Today, Norman wasn't going to allow it.

"Why are you here? You didn't come to apologize. The only thing you're sorry about is that you got burned. Your ego won't allow you to be sincerely sorry for anything. You wanted my business for the sole purpose of trying to make yourself look more professional while trying to take advantage of my success. Your greed outweighed any sort of family loyalty the second you forged my signature and then lied to my face about it. You took advantage the instant you heard I had memory loss. You'd do it again in a New York minute if you could. No, you're not sorry for any of it except maybe for the fact that you didn't come out smelling like a rose."

Norman felt a slight tap on his arm. It was Blake handing him a beer. Freddie looked to see if Blake had brought him a beer too—he hadn't.

As Blake slowly took a drink of his Dr. Pepper and Norman took a swig of beer, Freddie quipped, "I guess visitors don't warrant basic gestures of hospitality?"

"You're not my friend," Blake firmly asserted.

Norman smiled and rested his hand on Blake's shoulder. Just as Norman started to suggest it was time for Freddie to leave, Freddie blurted, "They arrested Brandi!"

Norman calmly took another sip of beer without showing any sign of surprise.

Freddie fidgeted slightly as he elaborated. "They say she murdered someone in a heist of some kind that she and Jian Henkel pulled off several years ago."

Eventually, Norman asked, "This Jian Henkel, is he related to the former owner of Too Perky Coffee?"

Freddie nodded. "Mireya is Jian's wife." He then briefly glanced towards the sky as if he were searching for an answer or some type of sign. "It was all Brandi's doing, you see? She's the one who pressured me into becoming your partner and then working to get you and Patrick to buy the coffeeshops." As he paused for a second, Norman and Blake slowly took another sip of their drinks. Neither showed any sign of emotion.

Growing frustrated with his failure to gain any visible sign of interest from his brother, Freddie started to plead more. "I had lost my job. I needed a rebound opportunity—a fresh start somewhere."

Norman nodded. "While all of that may be true, you didn't have to destroy my business to accomplish it. Regardless whether it was all your doing, or your failure to put your foot down with Brandi, it was still your fault. It was your ego—your pride—your greed."

Blake quietly finished his Dr. Pepper and walked back to the garage to continue his work.

Freddie stood quietly at first and then quipped, "I suppose I should feel lucky Brandi didn't try to frame me for murder like she had with Jian."

Norman replied, "If she really is a murderer, you should feel lucky she didn't kill you too! By the way, how did the police link her to a murder?"

"I guess it was all tied together. Mireya was trying to make a quick getaway when the feds swooped in and nabbed her. She figured Brandi had set her up to be arrested so Mireya flipped on Brandi. It seems like my wife and this Jian guy were con artists years ago, and one of their scams got out of hand, and a guy died. Mireya knew about it and used the information to get Brandi to do whatever she needed done."

Norman then asked, "How did the police find out about the coffeeshops' secret income source?"

"Oh, that. Well, a bunch of soccer moms had been protesting the shops because of their topless employees. After weeks of protesting, they started noticing odd behavior that they reported to the cops. The police staked out the shops and quickly learned what was going on."

Norman nodded his head and appeared to be pleased with hearing how the coffee shops got busted. Freddie looked slightly confused after seeing Norman's expression. Norman quickly quipped, "Soccer moms—saving the world one coffeeshop at a time."

In reality, Norman was just happy that Walter hadn't played a role in exposing the prostitution ring.

Sensing some of Norman's ice might have thawed, Freddie asked, "Can we work this out?"

Confused, Norman replied, "Freddie, if you hadn't tried to cheat me, destroy my business, lie to me, and treat me like a two-bit mark in some con game, I might feel sorry for you. As it is, I can only say now, it's not my circus, and you are certainly not my monkey!"

Stunned, Freddie could only say, "I just don't know what to do."

With a brief shake of his head, Norman responded, "Well, you'd better figure it out quickly since, regardless of her incarceration, Brandi still owns a quarter of your business and half of your debt. My advice to you is—get a good lawyer."

As Freddie began to say something else, a van pulled up, and three people got out. Norman called out to them. "The front door is open. Just start in the front two rooms for now. I'll be in shortly."

As the visitors waved acknowledgment, Freddie asked, "Who are they?"

Norman smiled briefly and then finished his beer before answering. "They are going to pack up the house for my move. I'm leaving here and starting over. I guess this means for the first time in your life, you'll be on your own. I will no longer be around to bail you out."

Shocked, Freddie stammered, "What? You're leaving? Where are you going? When..."

"NFA. Now, I think it's time for you to leave. I have a long list of things I need to get done today."

Confused, Freddie asked, "NFA?"

Norman had already turned his back and was walking towards the garage as he quipped over his shoulder, "No Forwarding Address. Goodbye, Freddie."

Inside, Blake held up an old 8-track player in one hand and a rusty boat anchor in the other as he said, "You could probably get money for this stuff."

"Well, if you want to set up a couple of tables in the yard and run a yard sale, I'll split the take with you."

"Fifty-fifty?"

"If you think that'd be fair."

Immediately, Blake started dragging stuff towards the sidewalk for his yard sale.

Meanwhile, Norman started rummaging through a box of stuff on the workbench. He was certainly in a purging frame of mind. He quickly viewed and discarded old photos. It was a toss-up as to which pictures were thrown away the quickest: pictures of his brother Freddie or pictures of Norman's ex-wife Adrianna and her son Dillon.

Suddenly, he came across a picture of Leila. He admired her smile and marveled at how little she'd changed since college. He thought about when they played music together. His reverie was broken by his ringtone. He quickly slid Leila's picture into his shirt pocket as he answered.

"Norman? This is Nigel Tilghma. I'm trying to reach Freddie. Do you know where he is?"

"You just missed him. He was here a few minutes ago."

"Well, darn it! I need to find out where he wants all of these railroad ties."

"Sorry—can't help you—not my concern."

"So, Norman, are you going to start up another business?"

Thinking for a second about his response, Norman replied, "Yes, I am starting a new business. I have already established an approved vendor list of suppliers that we'll be using exclusively.

Unfortunately, you're not on the list. Hope you track down Freddie about those railroad ties. Goodbye."

Norman smiled as he thought to himself, "That was very satisfying."

A woman's voice called out, "Hello—hello."

"Ms. Stuart, hello. What's up?"

"Please, call me Fay. I just wanted to ask your permission to add a couple of items to your yard sale."

"Certainly, Fay! However, don't be surprised if your son asks for a sizable commission for his efforts—I promised him half of whatever he makes."

Norman then asked, "Fay, may I ask what you do for a living?"

With a look of mild curiosity, she replied, "I'm a buyer for a construction company in Kent."

"Would you be interested in a new job?"

"No, thanks, though," She answered with a nervous laugh. "I'm really thinking about leaving the area. With all the crime and high taxes, it's just not the place I want to stay in."

Norman nodded his head in firm agreement. "The job would be in Ellensburg."

After an hour of discussion, Fay excitedly shook Norman's hand. "Sounds like we're moving to Ellensburg, too."

"Well, please don't tell your son until after the yard sale."

Later in the afternoon, Blake seemed to be doing a brisk business at his impromptu yard sale. At first, Norman paid little attention to being honked at from near the curb. After a second and third toot, Norman strained to see inside the car with the tinted windows. An arm motioned for him to come closer. As Norman slowly approached the car, he noticed it was Walter Polk.

He motioned to Norman to get in. As the door opened, the music came screaming out. "Why are you playing these oldies so loudly?"

"Get in—shut the door" was Walter's initial comment.

As Norman shut the door, he reached to turn down the music. Walter quickly remarked, "No, don't do that! My audio jammer is on the blink, so this is the next best thing."

"Audio jammer?"

"Yeah, over here, you never know who's listening in on your conversations."

"So, you just play your music really loud?"

"Not just any music. Certain old songs and some heavy metal work just as well as some of the middle-range jammers."

Norman was entertained by Walter's paranoia. "What brings you over to the west side of the mountains?" Norman bellowed.

"I came over to buy some computer equipment."

Norman interjected, "You know you could probably order this stuff online, and they could ship it to you."

Walter quickly replied, "There's no way I'm giving my mailing address to a complete stranger from Seattle!"

Norman just chuckled. "Hey, I need to ask you. You didn't have anything to do with breaking the story about the prostitution ring or directing the port authority to Freddie, did you?"

Walter flashed a quick smile as he quickly asked, "How'd you like your new website? If there's anything you don't like, we can change it in a blink of an eye."

Believing he wasn't going to get a straight answer from Walter, he allowed the topic of conversation to change to his new website and some tweaks he'd like to see.

As Norman was getting out of the car, he yelled over the music, "So, you stopped by just to say hi?"

"Oh, yeah, thanks for reminding me. Leila wants you to call her. She says you're not answering your phone. She knew I was nearby."

Norman laughed as he shut the door. Walter then rolled down the window and said, "Hey, Norman, those soccer moms are really quick to react to certain situations, aren't they?"

Before Norman could respond, Walter shouted, "See you on the other side of the pass," as he sped off.

Imagining the events between Walter and the soccer moms, Norman simply smiled and slowly shook his head.

After tending to a couple of matters with the packers and checking in on Blake's yard sale profits, Norman called Leila.

"Your personal messenger just told me that I needed to call you," he said as a greeting.

Leila laughed. "Well, if it's such an effort for you, don't bother!"

After bantering for a bit, she asked, "Can you be here by noon on Friday?"

"Sure. I think I could make it by then. Why? You taking me to lunch?"

"No, grab a snack on your way over. We have an appointment with the realtor to look at houses."

In a more serious tone, Norman replied, "Oh? We are joining a realtor to look for houses, are we?"

Leila dryly responded, "What's your point?"

With a playful air, Norman said, "I'm just curious as to when me looking for a new house became us looking for a new house."

Her reply summed it up. "You certainly don't think I'm going to let you get a place without my feedback, do you?"

Norman sighed. "I'm happy I don't have to go house-hunting by myself. I'm even happier that it'll be you by my side holding my hand through the process."

Leila snapped back, "I'll be by your side all right. Whether we're holding hands or not depends on how many decisions I get to make!"

ACKNOWLEDGEMENTS

I want to express my sincere appreciation for the knowledge, talent, and collaboration provided by my editor, Katherine Spivey of Alexandria, Virginia. She has been a tremendous partner throughout the process of writing my novels.

In addition, I want to acknowledge the talent and interpretation of Amanda Meyer of Seattle, Washington. She effortlessly took a verbal expression and transformed it into reality. Thank you for your artistic skill and graphic expertise. You can see more of her creations on Instagram.com/withwildhearts_co.

STAYING IN TOUCH

Readers can follow me at the flowing locations:

Facebook –
https://www.facebook.com/authorKeithKeltner/?ref=aymt_home
page_panel

Website –
https://k2-books.com/

Email –
keith.keltner@shymur.net

Linkedin –
https://www.linkedin.com/in/keith-keltner-5a428b1

Smashwords –
https://www.smashwords.com/profile/view/Shymur